Never Before Had Calco County Been Subjected to the Queries of a Medical Examiner

The well-run hospital was known across the country for its high standards and the caliber of its doctors. *But now its staff was facing the questions of a stern pathologist from the District Attorney's office* . . . and Dr. Prentice, Calco County's administrator, held only himself to blame.

He was a doctor of character, principle, and medical talent. But he was also a man who had gone against his better judgment. Dr. Prentice had submitted to the pressures of the Board of Directors, and accepted as resident physician Alden Vaizey, the nephew of Calco County's most powerful citizen.

Now he and his staff were facing a medical inquiry. *A young girl had died under mysterious circumstances* . . . and the medical examiner wanted to know WHY?

Had Carol Vincent died because of medical incompetence, or criminal negligence? Had Carol Vincent died because the attending doctor—Dr. Alden Vaizey —had failed to administer simple but life-saving treatment in time?

The
DOCTOR'S
PLEDGE

~~~ by ~~~

SHANE DOUGLAS

WILDSIDE PRESS

CHAPTER ONE

THE DOOR bore the legend "Dr. Stanley Prentice," and beneath it in larger lettering, "Medical Superintendent."

Dr. Glen Carew, Calco County Hospital's chief of surgery, read the words unconsciously. His mind was with a patient back in the Emergency Room who needed urgent surgery.

He opened the door. Dr. Prentice's secretary, Miss Iris Hilder, stopped her typing and sat forward, poised, waiting. Miss Hilder had been at County only a few months, but already she had become a legend in efficiency. She was neat blonde in her late thirties, and her blue eyes could deflate eager pharmaceutical salesmen with a single glance. And she was equally discerning with medical staff. A problem had to be real, and sticky, before it was carried through the closed door behind Miss Hilder for discussion and decision by Dr. Prentice.

Miss Hilder had had many years of experience in hospital administrative offices and had learned how to deal with querulous patients and relatives, salesmen, resident doctors and interns, nursing and domestic staff. She was expert at handling people, and on the secretarial side, her filing system was of the kind that brought out any reference Dr. Prentice ever needed and laid it on his overloaded desk in seconds. When she attended medical staff

5

and board meetings, she took notes in fast, accurate short-hand and kept the minutes of each meeting with the same precision with which she typed the hospital executive correspondence.

But nobody had ever seen Miss Hilder ruffled. Her clothes were always in good taste, well-cut, expensive. And her grooming was immaculate—make-up skillfully applied, every hair in place. She was always cool. Always self-assured. She looked, and was, the perfect secretary.

She smiled her approval at the man coming in now. Dr. Glen Carew was one of her favorites at County. He was a tall man and Miss Hilder noticed that he was slightly stooped, as though self-conscious about his height of six feet two. She admired his strongly handsome face—the way his dark brown eyes and very black brows and lashes contrasted with his unruly blond hair; the lines of strength at the corners of his mouth that went with the square chin with its deep cleft. It was a serious face, but it looked boyish now as he returned her smile.

"You wanted to see Dr. Prentice, Doctor?"

"Yes, Miss Hilder. If he's still here?"

Her eyes had noted Glen Carew's white hospital coat. "He'll be through in a few minutes, so you'd have time to change—that is, if you're going with him to the wedding."

Miss Hilder had the habit of finding out the reason before anyone walked through that door behind her.

He said, "Looks like I'm going to be late. Guy driving through to Reno rammed a truck a few miles downriver on one of the curves. Skidded right over the double center line. He was a D.O.A., but we've got the truck driver and the dead guy's wife and two kids in Emergency."

Sympathy for the innocent victims clouded her face. "Too bad! Especially today, with everyone who can be spared already off-duty for Dr. Flagg's wedding." It wasn't often that the overworked medical and nursing staff at County had a chance to relax, particularly Dr. Carew, and part of her sympathy was for him also. "Well," she said consolingly, "at least you might have a little unexpected help. Dr. Flagg's replacement is inside."

His eyes widened in surprise as she reached for the

intercommunication box on her desk. "I didn't know Dr. Prentice had decided on anyone."

"He'll tell you about it" she said, her glance at the closed door disapproving. She looked at her desk rather than at Glen Carew as Dr. Prentice's quiet voice spoke.

"Yes, Miss Hilder?"

"Dr. Carew is here, Doctor."

"Fine!" the muted voice from the other office said without hesitation. "I was just about to ask you to call him. Send Dr. Carew in."

She clicked off the intercom. "You're about to meet the new anesthesiologist in there. Dr. Alden Vaizey. He's coming in as a resident." Her tone was faintly derogatory. "Unless girls have changed he's going to cause a flutter among the nurses."

She was already typing again as Carew walked past. Her attitude puzzled him slightly. He knew that Miss Hilder had her favorites—Bill Randall, the darkly handsome assistant chief surgeon, was one, but it wasn't like her to show disapproval toward an untried newcomer. Miss Hilder was always fair.

Dr. Prentice stood up smiling as Carew came in. He was already dressed for the wedding. Slim, neat, his reddish hair streaked with gray but his eyes still young, he waved a hand toward the young man getting up quickly from a chair.

"Glen I want you to meet Alden Vaizey. Dr. Vaizey, this is Dr. Glen Carew, our chief of surgery. He's in charge of all things surgical, which includes anesthesia."

Carew studied the young man holding out his hand. Barely out of internship, he decided, returning the nervous handshake—perhaps a year of residency, at most. Twenty-eight maybe. Or thirty. Well dressed, and extremely good-looking, as Miss Hilder had suggested. Tall, slim, with glossy black hair, a thin black mustache, deep brown eyes and curling, black lashes. Hardly the athletic type, though. And probably sensitive. . . .

"I've heard a lot about you, Dr. Carew," he was saying. "I talked to Roy Flagg when I decided to apply here. I knew ⸺ in the East."

"You ⸺ together?"

"A bit. Roy was a resident—I was still an intern."

"And then?"

"Residency at a Chicago clinic until a couple of weeks ago. In surgery. But I've had a lot of experience with anesthesiology and I plan eventually to take my Boards in that field."

Carew nodded. "It's not an easy specialty." He smiled. "I would think Chicago would offer a wider range of experience—more action, so to speak—as any big city environment does. I gather you didn't find it so?"

"In the clinic they already had a very good man," Vaizey said slowly.

"Oh, yes. We had one here in Roy Flagg—" Carew began, but he was beginning to catch the drift of Vaizey's meaning.

"Yes, I know." Color flooded Vaizey's cheeks, making him look little more than a youth. "But Flagg's leaving here, and back in Chicago—well, the anesthesiologist there was a fixture. I thought I'd have a better future at Calco. You see, I was born here."

"Oh?" Carew had wondered at the name, if there was any connection between this young man and Calco's wealthiest family.

Alden Vaizey said quickly, "My father had the department store down on Humboldt. And others throughout Nevada. He died while I was at med school in the East."

"Our board chairman is Dr. Vaizey's uncle," Dr. Prentice put in dryly. "Incidentally, Dr. Vaizey says he doesn't mind starting at once. Which is fortunate, with Dr. Flagg being married this afternoon and so many of our medical staff wanting to look in briefly at either the church or the reception. Dr. Carew here is going along, Vaizey, so you could report to Dr. Lindemann when you're ready. He'll show you around. It would certainly help today if you could take Emergency—that is, if you're sure you don't want to wish Roy Flagg and his bride luck?"

Vaizey reddened. "I didn't know him that well, Doctor."

Prentice nodded. "Then report to Dr. Lindemann. He'll see that you get the things you need for diagnostic work. The floor nurses will tell you where to find anything else you might need. And one of the residents will always be within call somewhere on the floor if you need help."

"Yes, sir." Vaizey nodded to Carew, and gave his

friendly, flashing smile briefly from the door as he went out.

Prentice raised a questioning eyebrow. "Well, Glen?"

Carew shrugged. "Nice looking guy. And if you're starting him—he must be okay."

Dr. Prentice came around the desk, frowning. "That's just it, Glen. I didn't choose him."

"But you always hand-pick your medical staff." Carew looked at him, amazed. "That's why this place runs so Efficiently, even though, like every other county hospital in the country, we're understaffed. Why, there isn't a doctor here who'd refuse an extra duty if it was necessary, or grumble about it afterward. Not seriously, anyway. Each staff member fits in here, and each is a good man in his own line." Carew gestured with his hand. "Maitland in Pathology, Lindsay in Gynecology—"

"And Glen Carew in Surgery," Prentice broke in with a smile. "You're right, of course. I pick every staff member carefully. Each one appeared to me to be the best available choice, and there were always plenty. Only this time . . . it's a little different. Usually, I submit my choice to the Hospital Board and they accept it. This time there is only one applicant. Dr. Vaizey. His name was submitted to me by the Board."

"But—!" Carew stopped. "I see! The applicant's uncle?"

Prentice nodded. "Andrew Vaizey. Chirman of our Board and one of our biggest benefactors. He gave us twenty thousand last year toward new equipment for the OB wing, and the same amount the year before for surgical equipment. He'll give us another large donation this year for the latest anesthetic equipment. He promised the Board that at last night's meeting. He also reminded the Board that Vaizey's Department Store was one of the guarantors for our overdraft, and that a bequest in his brother's will endowed the Vaizey Wing over in OB with a substantial annuity."

Carew frowned. "Did Dr. Vaizey mention this?"

"No. Not a hint. He was grateful for the appointment—as the average young doctor would be. Right now, there are at least ten interns with their eyes on every residency available in a good hospital. And Calco County Hospital *is* good. We've made it that. Alden Vaizey is glad to be on our staff and in his home town. He knows he can move into a good practice in Calco without much trouble. The name of Vaizey carries weight here."

Carew said confidently, "Well, he seems likable enough, and he must have good credentials. Otherwise, no matter what pressure the Board brought to bear on you, he wouldn't be here."

"I didn't expect another Fellow of the American College of Surgeons," Prentice growled. "He got through medical school and internship. He has served three years of a surgical residency in Chicago, with emphasis on anesthesiology as a specialty. He's average, no better. I hope, no worse."

Carew opened his mouth to speak. The muted burr of the telephone stopped him. He was remembering all too clearly why he was here, that a patient waited.

Prentice said, as he reached for the phone. "Isn't it time you were getting ready for the wedding?"

"I came to ask you to excuse me. Indications are that the truck driver down in Emergency has a ruptured spleen. There's internal hemorrhage and shock. They're transfusing him now. I could be detained for hours. Depends on the result of our tests. That could be Lindemann now."

Dr. Prentice picked up the phone. "Yes?" he said. "Yes, Dr. Lindemann." He listened, then nodded to Carew. "Your patient's been transfused. They're taking him through now. Lindemann will have him in the O.R. in fifteen minutes. Kane has read the X rays and Maitland's tests confirm the diagnosis of a ruptured spleen." He spoke into the phone again. "Dr. Carew will be right up."

"I'll explain to Roy and Kristina," Prentice said as he hung up. He shook his head, his eyes troubled. "I can't blame Roy for resigning in favor of private practice. Especially now he's marrying Kristina Erickson. But I have a feeling we're going to miss him, Glen."

"I'm missing him already," Carew said ruefully. "On this case, I'll have to use Carter. Even if Vaizey was ready, I'd prefer to try him out on something easier than a splenectomy."

"Something like an ingrown toenail!" Prentice grunted. "Well, start him gently, Glen. It will be easier to evaluate his ability that way. Old Andrew believes the name of

10

Vaizey should be associated with Calco County Hospital more closely than through the Hospital Board or the checkbook. He wants Alden here as a *doctor*. So I'm being forced to give him his chance. Other than that, our new anesthesiologist gets no special privileges. I'll be watching him like a hawk, and if he isn't the man we want —out he goes."

"We'll soon know," Carew said. "I'll see you at the reception, maybe."

Carew walked with long strides toward the elevators. In Calco County Hospital, a patient's need always came first. It would always be that way. But, Carew couldn't help thinking as he passed the cluster of people around the Admitting Office on the ground floor, it always seemed busier whenever the staff hoped for a quiet afternoon. Like today, when everyone at County wanted to see the wedding of the popular anesthesiologist, Roy Flagg, to one of County's most popular R.N.'s, Kristina Erickson.

Most of those invited had already gone. A few, like Dr. Glen Carew, would be delayed by the present emergency, but almost everyone on the staff would be hoping for a chance to look in at the church, or later at the reception to wish the couple luck. For Dr. Flagg and his bride would be leaving Calco, and Calco County Hospital, immediately after their wedding.

Glen Carew was thinking about that now as he pressed the elevator button. He was going to miss Roy Flagg at the head of the operating table behind his screen, calling the readings of pulse, pressure, and respiration, the breath of the patient's life depending upon his skill with anesthesia as much as upon the skill of the surgeon carrying out the operation.

It wasn't going to be easy to work with another anesthesiologist after Flagg. He couldn't expect the new man to be as good. And Dr. Carter, now preparing the anesthetic machine up in the O.R. for the long, difficult operation that lay ahead, couldn't fill Roy's place either. Carter was only just through internship. He had been a resident in surgery only a few weeks, with four years of training ahead of him.

Carew's thoughts grew more troubled. Carter had been good as an intern, very good. And Carter, he was sure,

11

would have been interested in anesthesiology as a specialty if the Hospital Board had not decided to replace Flagg with someone else. Any time Carter had come in to watch an operation, he had watched the anesthesia rather than the surgery. And Roy Flagg had taught him many of the finer points of his specialty by precept and example. Carter would have made a good anesthesiologist. *Was* close to being one, right now. . . .

Carew stepped into the elevator. He must talk to Carter. The earnest young resident was too good a man to lose. Whatever he attempted he did carefully and well. He'd make a good surgeon. But if he had his heart set on a specialty in anesthesiology, County would lose him to some other hospital.

Carew didn't want that to happen. Just as he hadn't wanted to lose Roy Flagg. One missing member, and a closely knit team became less efficient. Perhaps that was why Dr. Prentice was so uneasy about Alden Vaizey. It wasn't solely the Board taking away his right of choice— Stanley Prentice was too good a medical superintendent to show pique at that. Or perhaps he was uneasy about Vaizey as a person—he didn't feel sure of the young doctor with the dazzling smile, the good looks, and the only average qualifications.

"They've sure got a sunny day for it, Dr. Carew, eh?" the elevator orderly said cheerfully.

"Yes, Sam," Carew agreed, knowing he meant the wedding of Roy Flagg and Kristina Erickson.

"Ain't going to seem the same around here," the elevator orderly remarked nostalgically. "Not without those two. Miss Erickson always smilin' and nice—and him with his good temper and his jokes."

"You can say that again, Sam."

"Well, good luck to 'em! I reckon Dr. Flagg will do pretty well down in L.A."

"He'll do well anywhere," Carew said, stepping out at the third floor.

In the scrub room, Carl Lindemann was already scrubbing, studying his thick arms carefully as he went through the ritual of ten-minute scrubbing with brush and ether soap. He peered up uncertainly as Carew greeted him,

12

lost without the thick bifocal glasses he had laid aside while he scrubbed.

"Anesthesia ready, Carl?"

Lindemann blinked at him myopically. "Yes, Dr. Carew. I checked Carter before I came in. Dr. Kane is setting up the X rays. Pathology reports everything is ready. Transfusion running, and a heparin drip as you ordered."

"Good! I'll join you inside. Is there an intern scrubbing in? If so, we'll use him on electrocautery."

"Moss came up from Emergency with me. He said he'd like to watch."

"Good. Have one of the nurses call him. I'll see you inside, Carl."

"Will I prepare the operative area?"

"Yes. Save as much time as you can."

Carew was already hurrying toward the doctors' locker room to don his scrub suit. He no longer thought of the new anesthesiologist or of Roy Flagg and his bride. He no longer thought of anything except the problem in major surgery that waited beyond the scrub room doors in the operating room.

In there, the patient breathed heavily in the beginning of anesthesia, with an anxious young Dr. Carter studying him over his mask behind the screen that separated the unsterile anesthesia equipment from the surgeons and their patient. The patient's head was beyond the curtain, and his body had already been draped in a sterile sheet, and sterile towels that at County were colored green like the surgeons' surgical gowns, masks, and caps.

Now only the operative area, bruised to a deep purple by the force of the blow that had ruptured the spleen, showed through the drapes. Lindemann finished sponging the swollen area of shaven skin with reddish antiseptic as Carew came in and studied the X rays in their view boxes along the wall.

The sponge went into the waste bucket, and in the silent operating room the tinkle of forceps sounded loud as they were dropped into the used surgical receptacle. Lindemann stepped back, waiting now, the responsibility no longer his as the surgeon moved into place across from him. Lindemann glanced automatically at the wall clock

13

that the circulating nurse was setting to time the operation.

"Miss Forrest?" Carew said, glancing at the masked and gloved scrub nurse wheeling her Mayo stand of prepared surgical instruments into place over the operating table and the patient's legs.

"Ready, Dr. Carew." She looked at him encouragingly above her mask. She had beautiful eyes, of a soft, clear gray, beneath dark brows and lashes. More than once, before a difficult operation, the calm, steady look in those eyes had given him strength for the task ahead. He was glad she was with him now. He looked over the screen at Dr. Carter.

Kathie Forrest was a close friend of Kristina Erickson's. Just as he was of Roy Flagg's. They had planned to drive to the wedding together, and should have been getting ready right now, but here they were, both caught by the emergency.

"Ready, Dr. Carew," Carter said nervously.

Carew waited for a long moment before he asked mildly, "Pressure?"

"B.P. is sixty over thirty, Doctor," Carter said, red above his mask. "He's in shock."

That was obvious. Carew said gently, "That's going to be your worry for the next hour or so, Dr. Carter. Keep him on oxygen. Give me plenty of readings. Pulse, pressure, and respiration. How is he in that department now?"

Carter gave the readings quickly, his flush deepening. He was a tall young man with fair hair like Carew's hidden beneath his surgical cap, and honest blue eyes that darkened in concentration now.

"Constant reports," the surgeon said. "Keep him oxygenated. Keep his reflexes obdurated. I want to know about any change in pulse, respiration, or B. P. immediately. Right?"

"Yes, sir."

"Let's go. Miss Spain, move the electrocautery in closer for Dr. Moss. Lindemann will tell you when we need the pump. We're going to have to aspirate away a lot of blood in there. Constant drip with the heparin. Right, everyone? Scalpel, Miss Forrest."

It came into his hand smoothly, and this time he did

not see the scrub nurse as a woman. He saw only the scalpel.

The taut skin within the open square of the operative area, scarlet and bruised purple in its frame of sterile green towels, looked like an overripe fruit that might burst as the knife touched it. It had been rigid before under the control of muscles that had tightened instinctively against pain, as hard as a board to the pressure of his fingers. Now, anesthesia had relaxed the muscles, allowing that upper left quadrant of abdomen to thrust outward with the pressure of the hemorrhage within.

Carew glanced at Lindemann. "We'll tie off as we go once we enter the cavity, Doctor. Cautery for small bleeders he can do without. Clip any vessels that give us trouble in the superficial layers before we open the cavity. We'll tie them off as we close."

Lindemann nodded heavily, frowning in concentration as his mind showed him the clinical picture. He thought slowly, but was thorough. Carl Lindemann would never make a really good surgeon, but he was a very competent assistant. He obeyed instructions to the letter with Teutonic precision.

Lindemann had liked Roy Flagg and Kristina Erickson. But he was happier to take the place of someone else here rather than go to their wedding. Away from his work, Lindemann liked the seclusion of his room in the residence, and his books. He had found peace here at Calco County Hospital after the long torture of war and persecution in the Germany of World War II.

He was content to be left alone.

He watched the line of red well from the first skin incision. He held out his hand to Kathie Forrest for a hemostat as the first bleeder, under pressure from the swelling hemorrhage within, spurted a line of tiny red spots across Dr. Glen Carew's green surgical gown.

He clamped ponderously, squinting against the glare of light above the table.

Balancing the oxygen in the closed circuit general anesthetic against the patient's need, Carter called the readings of pressure, pulse, and respiration. The youthful doctor was doing a good job behind his screen, his eyes

15

never still as he checked the patient's condition constantly, trying to remember all the things that Roy Flagg had taught him. But somehow his concentration kept slipping. He kept thinking of the new anesthesiologist, whom rumor said was even now at the hospital and ready for work.

What did you have to do to get the breaks you wanted? Anesthesiology was a well-paid specialty which so many interns passed over when they became residents and began to plan their permanent future. Carter had known for a long time that he wanted to be an anesthesiologist. Roy Flagg had encouraged his ambition, had praised his ability more than once.

So where had that gotten him at County? Maybe he should resign and take up a residency someplace else, where they could offer him the chance he wanted. . . .

"Dr. Carter?" Carew's voice said sharply beyond the curtain.

He flushed guiltily as he reached hurriedly to press the carotid pulse at the base of his patient's throat.

"B.P. still sixty over thirty, Doctor. Respiration is shallow."

"Pulse?"

Flustered, he lost count, and had to start over.

"I suggest you take the reading from the sphygmograph," Carew's calm voice said.

"Yes, sir! Of course!"

He gave the reading, stumbling over his interpretation of it. Even an intern should have remembered that there was a sphygmograph strapped to the patient's wrist—that with a splenectomy the left arm was raised, the wrist and hand in plain view on the anesthetist's side of the curtain. There had been no need to check the pulse at the carotid artery, as he had been attempting to do. Angry and confused, he went back to his chart and his dials.

Beyond the curtain, Dr. Carew had deepened the longitudinal incision which started high up at the diaphragm on the left side, and came straight down to a little above the naval. He had cut through skin and connective tissue. He had turned the scalpel with the layers retracted and made a transverse incision across the left rectus muscle and fasciae to expose the contents of the abdomen.

16

The operation continued in silence now, except for an occasional word that brought sponge or instrument or ligature into the hands of the surgeon and his assistant from the scrub nurse. The splenic artery was ligated, the aspirator emptied of the dark blood of hemorrhage from the ruptured spleen. Miss Spain, the chief operating room nurse, drew the suction machine back a little.

Carew blunt-dissected the injured spleen away from its adherence to surrounding structures. His gloved fingers probed up under the cage of the ribs, out of sight, gently clearing adhesions of thin membrane away. He could feel the rupture against the palm of his hand, cupped to contain the break lesion without further bursting open the spleen.

"Is it clearing?" Lindemann asked anxiously, ready with forceps holding a large gauze pad soaking in normal saline.

"It's clearing."

Carew was drawing out the spleen, bringing it down beneath the cage of ribs, delivering it into the gaping wound held open by blunt retractors. Purplish, oozing dark blood through the ruptured membrane that formed its outer skin, the ruptured spleen came into sight slowly.

Carew drew it out carefully until he could see the pedicle, the stalk of the fan-shaped group of blood vessels that nourished it.

The preoperative injection of epinephrine had shrunk the spleen considerably, bypassing at least some of its blood content into circulation. Blood had oozed into the cavity and surrounding tissues through the rupture. Diminished in size, the spleen was easier to handle now.

Working, Carew felt less anxiety for his patient. The man breathing stertorously into the rebreathing bag beyond the anesthetist's screen could live a useful life again soon. Other reticuloendothelial cells would take over the function of the missing spleen. In a couple of months, he would be driving his truck again.

Carew glanced up at the wall clock. Almost three! In a few minutes, Roy Flagg would be watching a radiant Kristina walk toward him down the aisle.

His eyes met those of the scrub nurse as he turned his head, and he read the same thought in them. But those

17

gray eyes seemed only to mirror content that she was here, assisting him.

Glen Carew studied the operative field. They were going to be late, even for the reception. The slow processes of the operation were still to be carried out: the careful dissection of the small vessels that had nourished the spleen . . . the separation and clamping of the veins of the vasa brevia . . . the separation of the pedicle from the tail of the pancreas. All of it was delicate, slow surgery.

At least there were no accessory spleens that must be found and removed lest they grow to gigantic proportions —as there might have been if the spleen had been diseased instead of ruptured.

The surgeon's head bent again to identify and separate the first small vessel. . . .

CHAPTER TWO

DAN WARD, M.D., one of County's interns, drew deeply on his cigarette and stared out the window of the small surgeons' office adjoining the Emergency Room. Across the lawns an aged sedan had stopped outside the nurses' residence, and a group of student nurses were climbing inside. He recognized the intern who was driving.

"Off to the wedding," his friend Jim Keaton remarked laconically. "Boy, what wouldn't I give to be nursing one of those chicks on the back seat, Dan!"

"I'd have been doing that little thing, if Lindemann hadn't decided he might need two interns in Emergency tonight. Why couldn't he have been satisfied with just you?" Thin, dark-haired, his brown eyes angry, Ward stubbed his cigarette with an angry gesture.

"Well, we were both needed earlier, when the road accident people were brought in," Keaton said soberly. "Lindemann's a slow guy, but he seems to have an extra sense that warns him when trouble's coming."

"Sure," Ward said, staring at a pretty blonde who just managed to squeeze into the overcrowded jalopy. "But why *me?* Why not Moss?"

"Moss scrubbed for the splenectomy."

"Yeah," Ward said spitefully. "I should've thought of that myself. Lindemann asked me about it, but I said no

19

thanks! How did I know the old guy was going to put me in Emergency with him for the rest of the day?"

"If it's any consolation, I'm stuck there with you." Keaton sighed. Unlike the thin, intense Ward, he was solidly built, with sandy hair and rather pale blue eyes, and a thick band of freckles across his nose. "Moss should be through in the O.R. pretty soon."

"So where does that get me!" Ward said disgustedly. His face brightened at a sudden thought. "Hey, maybe I can grab Moss when he's through up there, and persuade him to change!"

"Worth a try," Keaton conceded. "He isn't very bright. But I doubt if he's that dumb either. He did say something about going downtown."

"Downtown!" Ward sneered. "What's downtown for Moss? A movie maybe? A beer or two by himself? He isn't interested in girls, just in surgery. Now me, I wouldn't waste my off-duty time like that. Did you see the blonde? The last one to get into Reynolds' car? I'd find her. Those kids are only going to the church. After that, nothing—unless some Galahad comes along with a proposition. Like a show maybe, a drink, a slow drive home . . ."

"That costs."

"So what? I've got twenty."

"You have? Well, how about that five you owe me?"

The phone on the desk burred abruptly, cutting across Keaton's voice. Ward picked it up quickly.

"Dr. Ward here. Yes?"

The thin, harsh voice of the Chief R.N. in Emergency stabbed back at him. "We have an emergency coming in, Dr. Ward. A woman, about twenty. Collapsed in a telephone booth outside Vaizey's. She's hemorrhaging badly, the ambulance driver says. We can expect her here in ten minutes."

Ward's eyes were alert. "What sort of hemorrhage, Miss Flint? Arterial? Has she been involved in an accident?"

"Isn't that for you to find out, Doctor?" Miss Flint's voice was acidulous. "I can't see her from here, and that is all the information I have. It's a hemorrhage, and an emergency." The phone clicked down.

"One of these days," Ward told the empty phone, "I'm going to try to get blood out of a flint."

"Yeah." Keaton clapped him on the shoulder. "She gets me that way too. Come on!" He'd forgotten all about getting his five back from Ward now. He thought only of the emergency.

"If it's severe hemorrhage, she should call a resident, not us," Ward muttered angrily as they left the room. "Who the hell does she think she is, the sarcastic way she orders us around? Anyway, why not send this patient to Gynecology? You can bet what it is."

"Because (a) regulations say that a patient needing urgent attention must first pass through the Emergency Room before being sent to any other department of the hospital. And (b) because here at Calco County Hospital the same as anywhere else, a head nurse is far, far higher in the social scale than a lowly intern. Any more questions, *Doctor?*"

"Go to—!" Ward broke off as they walked through into the vestibule of the Emergency Room. Miss Flint was standing beside a nervous duty nurse at the admitting desk, talking to a tall young man in hospital whites with a stethoscope tucked into the pocket like a badge of office. "Say, who's that?" he whispered.

"Search me!" Keaton said. "Unless it's the new intern come to take Carter's place, Carter now being a resident. What do you think?"

"Seems old for an intern. And Flint sure isn't treating him like one—look at her preening her feathers."

The stranger looked around as they came up and eyed them without great interest. "You two the duty interns? I'm Vaizey, new anesthesiologist here. I'm helping out in Emergency today while some of the other residents go to the wedding. I was told to report to Dr. Lindemann, but Miss Flint says he's operating."

"Third floor," Ward said. "Ruptured spleen. Dr. Carew is operating—Dr. Lindemann assisting."

Vaizey nodded. "I'll take over here until Dr. Lindemann comes down. Which is Ward and which Keaton?"

"I'm Ward," the dark-eyed young intern said, woodenfaced. He was deciding that he wasn't going to like the new resident. Mostly, the residents at County treated the

21

hospital's interns as equals, or almost so. And if they were exacting at times, you learned from the experience. As a medical student Ward had met residents at other hospitals like Vaizey. They rode interns ragged, on the principle that they'd lived through the same thing as interns themselves. If the treatment hadn't harmed *them,* it wasn't going to harm Dr. John Intern Doe, or anyone else.

Only they dished it out much tougher than they'd had it, with a perverse satisfaction.

So Ward watched Dr. Alden Vaizey's supercilious smile in silence and waited to be insulted.

"I presume you two have some elementary knowledge of medicine," Vaizey said contemptuously. "Anything past that, call me. I'll be in the office there."

"How d'you like that?" Ward demanded as the resident casually strolled away in the direction of the office they'd just vacated.

"Easy, Dan," Keaton said. "It's just the way he's built."

"I'd like to rearrange him!"

"Don't let it tempt you. Vaizey, he said? Isn't the Board Chairman a Vaizey? You reckon that's just coincidence?"

"Huh?" Ward said, startled. He walked over to where Miss Flint was supervising the preparation for the incoming hemorrhage. Keaton followed him slowly.

Miss Flint looked up. "Yes, Doctor?"

"I was wondering if you told Dr. Vaizey there was an emergency hemorrhage coming in, Miss Flint?"

"I have, and we're preparing for it, Doctor."

"Someone ready to rush a blood sample away for matching?"

Since that was hardly worth answering, Miss Flint merely looked at him and nodded.

"No further details, of course?" Ward went on tentatively. The Chief R.N. in Emergency always made him feel a fool. "Or anything about her blood group? She'll probably need urgent whole-blood transfusion."

"They never have their blood type," Miss Flint said tartly.

"They should all be made to carry a card or something with their type on it. Save lives. By the way, Miss Flint,

22

our new resident wouldn't happen to be related to the Board Chairman—Vaizey's Department Store and all that?"

Miss Flint's thin lips compressed. She glanced at the closed door of the small office, fighting an impulse that urged her to tell the waiting intern to go ask Dr. Vaizey. But she was a woman, and being first with an item of gossip, even to a lowly intern, had its satisfaction. So she told him, just the way she had heard it from Miss Harris who operated the switchboard and who was also the greatest source of information in Calco County Hospital.

She was still talking when they heard the wail of the ambulance siren out in the street, followed by the squeal of brakes, the throwing of gravel outside. Then there was no time for gossip.

The woman on the stretcher now being wheeled quickly through into the Emergency Room lay on her side, writhing slowly, her legs drawn up, teeth bared. Her pallor held the gray tinge of the death she was fighting with those slowly writhing movements. The blanket slipped down, showing a blood-soaked dress and shoes. Small moaning sounds escaped between the clenched teeth; her eyes were open, the pupils pinpointed by pain.

Ward's eyes were grim. "What's the story?"

"We got a police call," the ambulance man explained. "She was lying in a phone booth. There was a lot of blood. There's a store credit card in her bag identifying her as Carol Vincent, address, Seventy-two Harker. It's an apartment house. Mostly young women live there who work in the offices or stores around town. The card says she's a Miss."

"Relatives notified?"

"The police are trying to find them. She wasn't involved in any accident that's been reported. Vaginal bleeding. We couldn't stop it."

Ward held up the blanket. "Uterine hemorrhage!" he said, tight-faced. "Get her into the examination room. Miss Flint, needle for a blood sample—No! Her veins will have collapsed! Break out gloves. A sample of the blood she's losing will be quicker."

Ward was following the stretcher. Keaton caught him up. "Miscarriage?" he asked in a low voice.

"What do *you* think, with this hemorrhage? Or abortion. Maybe a criminal one. Get Dr. Vaizey on the jump, Jim. Ask him to call someone down from Gynecology. Tell him it's an emergency."

Keaton hurried away, as the duty nurse and Miss Flint lifted the girl off the low stretcher onto the examination table. Ward drew on gloves quickly, took the blood sample.

"Tell them to rush it for type! Bring back a flask of whole blood!"

His face was pale as he fastened the blood-pressure cuff on a limp arm that tried weakly to resist his efforts.

"Lie still! Lie still, please, **Miss Vincent**," Ward pleaded. "Miss Flint, get me a cutdown set . . . a needle . . . saline." He looked around anxiously. What the hell was keeping Vaizey, he wondered.

The sounds coming from between the girl's clenched teeth grew louder. Became coherent . . .

"Don't—! Please don't—!"

Ward stared at the blood pressure reading. Sixty over thirty. And falling! What now? Save time . . . get ready to transfuse. . . .

"Here, Dr. Ward," Miss Flint's voice said behind him. She had brought the cutdown set.

"Hold her!" he ordered.

The ankle beneath Ward's hand held the chill of death. He made the small incision that opened a vein, and dropped the knife to get rid of it quickly, before pinching the opening closed. "Blankets. Two blankets. Cover her from the waist up. Miss Flint, oxygen!"

Ward glanced at the door as he secured a tube in the open vein with sutures. Where the hell *was* Vaizey?

He fastened the tube in place with sure fingers. He ordered Miss Flint to move the stand closer. He started a saline drip. He added ergot to contract the uterus in an effort to stop the hemorrhage.

And then there was no more to be done, except to wait and watch while Miss Flint gave the woman intermittent oxygen. Ward looked at the patient for the first time as a woman.

Except for lips that looked overbright with lipstick that she had smeared in pain, her skin had the bloodless

24

transparency that went with the fluttering, diminishing pulse. She was young. Dark hair was plastered to her forehead with cold sweat, and her brown eyes were only a mirror of pain and shock.

They were trying to focus on Ward now, as she attempted to speak. He bent closer quickly.

"Yes?"

"Help . . . me! Please . . . help me!"

"I'm trying, Miss Vincent. But you must lie still, don't be frightened or resist us."

"I am frightened . . . because . . . I know . . . I'm dying. . . ." Her agonized eyes appealed to Ward to deny that. He forced a smile.

"We're going to transfuse you in a minute. You'll start to feel better then."

"No!" She said it clearly, with unexpected strength. "No! No! You mustn't!" A contraction came then, silencing her as Miss Flint's hands held her upper body still against the contraction.

"But you must have transfusion," Ward said.

"No! No . . . I can't . . . anger God anymore! I can't allow you to give me . . . another person's blood!"

Ward straightened. "Are you trying to tell me that transfusion is against your religious beliefs?"

"Yes! Yes—it's better that I die!"

Ward stared at her, uncertain now, forcing himself to remember the legal implications. But she seemed to have forgotten him suddenly.

"It wasn't a baby . . ." she whispered. "Not yet it wasn't. . . . And he said he'd help me. He said . . . there'd be no trouble . . . no pain."

"Who said?" Ward bent again. "Who did this?"

Her brown eyes looked toward him in a glazed, unseeing stare.

"God forgive me . . ." she moaned. "I didn't realize . . . Oh, God!"

"Who did this to you?" Ward demanded, his voice rising unconsciously in anger. "Who?"

"*Dr. Ward!*"

Ward turned quickly, his anger still upon him. Alden Vaizey was standing just inside the door of the examination room, his eyes fixed on the patient. Behind him, the nurse Ward had sent hurrying away with the blood sample was trying to get back in with the first flask of whole blood. Noticing her impatience, Ward had the impression that Vaizey had been watching him for some time.

"Nurse, get that flask in here!" he said curtly. "Is someone coming over from Gynecology, Doctor?"

Vaizey stepped aside to let the nurse in, but he came no closer to the girl on the examination table. "Dr. Lindsay is not in the hospital," he told Ward, without altering the fixed stare. "The other doctors on Gynecology are all with patients. I'm taking over here until Dr. Lindemann can come down from surgery."

"Then let's get her transfused," Ward said impatiently.

"I just heard the patient tell you that transfusion is against her religious beliefs."

"If she isn't transfused, she'll die!" the intern protested.

"I said I'm taking over here, Ward," Vaizey snapped. "What has been done?"

"I've started a saline drip. Ergot to contract the uterus. We're treating her for shock. But what she needs right now is whole blood. We can't wait for Dr. Lindemann to get here."

"If you transfuse someone against their will, against their religious beliefs, Ward, they usually suffer great emotional conflict. The psychological damage is irreparable. Gloves, Miss Flint. I'll examine her."

"You're wasting time!"

"Since you seem so anxious, Doctor Ward," Vaizey said, "go call another doctor. I've no objection to a second opinion—provided it's qualified."

"I'll call Dr. Carew!" Ward said furiously.

"Carew has left the building," Vaizey said shortly. "I watched him drive out the gates just now. Dr. Lindemann should be down soon." He had the gloves on, but his eyes still watched the girl on the bed. "She seems to have lapsed into coma, Miss Flint. What's her blood pressure now?" He moved closer, belatedly.

"Systolic pressure is under sixty. Diastolic pressure barely twenty, Doctor."

"She'll have *none* if you don't transfuse her," Ward

26

said bitterly, and strode out. He ran blindly down the passage, seeing only a young woman's strained face, the bright slash of smeared lipstick. She must have been hemorrhaging for hours.

Ward snatched up the phone in the office. Help had to be summoned for the dying girl before it was too late.

In the examination room, Dr. Alden Vaizey was examining the girl on the table.

"Her pulse is failing, Doctor," Miss Flint observed anxiously. "Diastolic pressure is almost gone. It's too low to get a reading now!"

He nodded and murmured something. He straightened from palpating the abdomen. He looked paler. The gray eyes that Miss Flint had admired when she met him a short while ago were suddenly almost black. She watched him curiously.

"Are you all right, Doctor?"

He avoided her inquiring gaze. "Did the patient say anything about how this happened?" His voice was shocked.

"Nothing! Dr. Vaizey, don't you think we should transfuse?" She glanced at the door, hoping that Dan Ward would hurry his call, that Dr. Lindemann would come in, or Dr. Maitland—anyone! But Dr. Vaizey's expression changed suddenly.

"Change the flask. Quickly," he said, staring down. "The whole blood. I'll take the responsibility! It's a tubal pregnancy, ruptured. . . ."

Miss Flint had seldom moved so fast. Her expert fingers changed the flasks, adjusted the drip. A part of her mind told her that the transfusion should be under pressure—that it was already too late for a normal transfusion—that if Dr. Lindemann were here he would have had a pressure transfusion running long since.

But the drip started at last. Miss Flint looked anxiously at the girl, and her thin lips compressed tightly.

It *was* too late, eve for a pressure transfusion. The young woman's body was arching as she struggled against asphyxiation. Sweat beaded on her forehead. Her lips were turning blue.

"Oxygen," Vaizey said urgently. He got the mask himself before Miss Flint could reach it. His fingers flew on

27

the valves. But the girl was breathing with gasps that weakened, stopped. Her head stiffened. Her eyes opened, changing, becoming filled with terror.

"I didn't . . . mean it!" she gasped. "Oh God!"

The open eyes rolled, her head fell back. The sound of her panting was gone.

Watching her, Miss Flint was aware that the new resident was turning away, walking toward the door. He went out without speaking.

"Doctor?" she called sharply. But he didn't look back.

Miss Flint glanced at the time automatically, her mind recording it for the report. She came around the examination table to press down the lids over those frightened eyes, shutting off the fear and guilt which had seemed indelibly frozen there. Miss Flint was conscious of Dr. Lindemann's heavy footsteps hurrying toward the room as she gently laid the dead girl's body flat and straight.

CHAPTER THREE

"FOR AWHILE there, I figured we wouldn't even make the reception," Glen Carew said, turning his car into the crowded parking lot. "But I kept hoping, and we're here."

"Guess I broke all records changing my clothes," the girl beside him said, laughing.

Carew switched off the ignition. "I haven't even had time to tell you that you look lovely, Kathie. But then, you always do."

Kathie Forrest was glad that in the semidarkness of the interior of the car he couldn't see her face clearly. She had flushed right up to her hairline at the compliment—although the way he had said it hadn't made it sound like a compliment. It was more like the way he'd remark, "Your color is better this morning," to some patient.

She would have liked a little more feeling in his voice. In fact, right now, having caught her breath after the rush to shower and don the glamour that went with her new corn-colored Thai silk frock, she suddenly felt she would like to be kissed.

"Thank you, Doctor." She matched his noncommittal tone.

"Hey, the next thing you know I'll be holding out my hand for an instrument."

She laughed dutifully. Through the wide windows of

the hotel where the reception was being held she could see the tables, and pick out familiar figures sitting there. She saw Roy Flagg's red hair and caught a glimpse of Kristina's radiant face as she looked up at him. Kathie was glad that Kristina had not asked her to be maid of honor, that she had chosen one of her former friends from Bellevue.

"Looks like County's old home week, Glen," she remarked.

"Sure does!" Studying Kathie's profile, he resisted an impulse to kiss her. Perhaps later, he thought, and was surprised as he recognized this intent. It made him feel more human, even though it drove him out of the car and around to open the door for her. It meant that the tensions of the hospital had been left behind. He was glad suddenly that he was here with Kathie Forrest. Especially glad that it *was* Kathie he was with tonight.

"Let's go!" he said.

He felt proud of her as they walked inside. Beside him, she looked small, even with her regal walk. A red-haired girl with steady gray eyes. Looking lovely, as he had told her so bluntly before. Lovely in any surroundings, in any circumstances. Even in an operating room, wearing a shapeless surgical gown and concealing mask.

But tonight Kathie was especially beautiful in the gold color which highlighted her hair and eyes. Her figure had turned the head of many a male patient when she walked through the wards in her starched hospital uniform. Neither uniform nor scrub dress could conceal those pert breasts, nor hide from male imagination the slender legs, the woman's body that the well-cut dress flattered now.

Carew led her around to rejoice with the bride and groom, aware that almost everyone was looking their way, the male glances for Kathie. Nobody in the big room could overshadow Kathie—not even the bride, looking absolutely radiant in her white wedding gown, her fair hair piled smoothly in a high chignon above the tiara of pearls that held her billowing veil in place.

He was glad when they sat down together at a nearby table, although he could not have explained why other men's interest in Kathie should annoy him.

Bill Randall, Carew's darkly handsome assistant, greeted them delightedly.

"We'd about decided you two had taken the wrong turning and lost yourselves across the river—until Dr. Prentice came in and explained. How went the splenectomy?"

"No complications." Carew smiled. "Made us miss the ceremony at the church, but thank heaven we could make the reception."

"Glad you did, Glen! Oh, and this is Val. Valerie Cassidy—Kathie Forrest and Dr. Glen Carew. Now don't search your memory, you two. Val *isn't* a nurse."

The girl was blonde and very pretty. Carew talked to her as Randall organized drinks for them. Together with Kathie, he moved into the spirit of the evening.

"What's wrong with nurses?" Dr. Jimmy Woldman was asking from across the table, where he sat with his fiancée, the petite and attractive nurse, Jane Barry.

"Nothing, when they look like Jane or Kathie," Randall said, laughing. "Or Mrs. Roy Flagg over there. But some luckier guy always seems to get the pick of the crop."

Tonight, Bill Randall was remembering another girl who had been a nurse but was now a rancher's wife. If he closed his eyes, he knew he'd see her face again, and feel the way he had when he'd been in love with her. If weddings made him feel like this, he decided, he was going to skip the next one he was invited to. He glanced past Carew at Kathie Forrest, and the bitter twist his lips had acquired suddenly, relaxed. Unless it happened to be the wedding of Glen and Kathie. He'd go to that one, by God! If it ever came off. If Glen ever relaxed enough to allow himself to fall in love. . . .

He turned back abruptly to the blonde girl beside him and picked up his drink.

"Still worried about your friend, Valerie?"

She looked up quickly. It was her first date with Bill Randall, and she knew that she should feel flattered by his interest, that he had asked her to come. He was awfully good-looking in a manly kind of way. Only tonight . . .

"I'm sorry, Bill—I just can't get her out of my mind."

31

"To heal sometimes, to relieve often, to console always. That's my motto. You can tell Bill."

"Well, she was sick."

"Send her along to County. I'll attend her with my very best bedside manner—on your behalf, of course! What seems to be the matter with her?"

Her eyes avoided his. "I don't know. Just tired and out of sorts, I guess. She was . . . very depressed."

Randall grinned. "Fairly normal symptoms. She could be in love."

She glanced at him quickly to see if his words held a double meaning. But his glass was being filled again. She looked across at the beautiful bride whose deep blue eyes shone with happiness as she talked with her parents, her red-haired husband beside her looking down at Kristina with a proprietary air that would have been comical if it hadn't held so much undisguised tenderness and pride.

She sighed. Some girls were lucky. For others it never worked out. Like Carol. She was almost certain that Carol was pregnant.

"Then, when she didn't come home last night . . ." Valerie left it at that.

Randall sipped his drink. "Love could still be the diagnosis, you know. She could be with the boy friend."

"She's only been in Calco a few weeks. She came from Illinois. She doesn't seem to go out much at all, except to visit with me. And I live next door."

"No male visitors?"

"None that I know about."

"Mystery girl," Randall said. "Pretty?"

"Very. Brunette."

"Uh-huh. At the moment, I prefer blondes. Blondes with green eyes like yours. Cute . . ." He realized she wasn't falling in with his light-hearted banter. "Where does your friend work?"

Valerie frowned. "She doesn't. But don't get the wrong idea. She has money of her own. She dresses well. The other day when I met her downtown I saw a dress I liked at Vaizey's. She offered to lend me sixty to buy it."

"Huh?" he said. "An heiress maybe! She didn't mention anything about a date last night?"

"No. She was out when I came home from the office.

And she didn't come home last night. I looked in this morning when the maid was tidying her apartment. Carol's bed hadn't been slept in."

Randall made another attempt to shake away his companion's gloom. "Well, it's my bet she's home now, and wondering where you've gotten to."

"No. I told her I was going out this afternoon, and that I might be late."

"Truer words were never spoken," Randall said with a wicked grin.

Valerie Cassidy ignored his remark. She knew how to look after herself. She wasn't like Carol. And besides, Bill was a doctor, wasn't he? A funny kid, Carol. Shy, sensitive, underneath a bit religious. But Carol had gotten herself pregnant, she was almost sure of that. It didn't pay a girl to be too unworldly, too innocent.

"Seriously," Bill Randall said then, "if your friend isn't back tonight, maybe we should try to find out what's happened. Or ask the police."

She looked at him appealingly. "Will you help me, Bill? Really? I am worried. Carol's such a nice kid."

"If you say so," he said cynically.

"I do say so," she said angrily. "She is nice. No matter what—" She broke off. She had almost blurted out that she suspected pregnancy, almost told Bill Randall of her fear that Carol might have done something desperate. That she could be dying somewhere. Even be dead. . . . She had almost blurted that out right here at the wedding. She was close to tears.

"Hey, there," Bill Randall said in a low voice. "Sure, she's nice, if you say so. If she's your friend—she has to be. That's all I meant, Val. I'll help you find her, just as soon as the reception is over. I'll start right now by asking Dr. Carew if she's been admitted at County as a casualty. Only I'm pretty sure that no young women were admitted through Emergency last night or today. At least not before I left. I would have heard."

Her lips trembled, but she was looking at him gratefully. His gray eyes held real sympathy. He meant what he said. He was going to help her to find Carol.

"Thanks, Bill!" she said in a soft voice. "You're awfully nice."

His eyes were crinkling again at the corners. His flippancy came back. "People tell me that all the time," he said. "It's getting so I almost believe it. Say, what's your friend's name?"

"Carol Vincent."

He leaned over to speak to Glen Carew. She held her breath as Carew considered. She watched him shake his head.

Her worry returned, stronger.

Glen Carew was enjoying himself. He hadn't really expected to. He had come to the wedding as a duty, because he liked both the bride and the groom, and had played a small part in bringing them together once when their romance had threatened to break up.

It hadn't occurred to him that he could enjoy himself at a wedding. But he had never felt as free from care, as free from the *hospital,* since student vacation days.

Dancing with Kathie, while Roy Flagg and Kristina were changing into their going-away clothes, was an unexpected delight. He had never been a really good dancer, and in recent years his dancing had been limited to the annual hospital ball when he danced with Mrs. Prentice, Miss Godsell, the Director of Nurses, and one or two nurses as the occasion made it necessary.

But dancing with Kathie Forrest was something different. He was aware of her nearness, the way his blood was pulsing strongly. He stifled resentment when Jimmy Woldman claimed her, and waited with open impatience until she hurried back to him, her gray eyes wide and shining.

When Roy Flagg came back with Kristina, they were immediately separated and encircled by friends. Glen Carew lost Kathie then to the group of nurses around Kristina.

He was standing alone when Max Addison's deep voice said beside him, "And this is no damned place for any self-respecting bachelor who wants to stay that way."

Carew turned good-humoredly toward the burly pilot who flew the flying ambulance plane that served County Hospital. Theirs was a long and friendly association that had covered mercy flights to almost every corner of northern Nevada.

34

"I would have said the prognosis was good so far as you're concerned, Max." He glanced around. "But don't tell me you were so scared you came alone?"

"Not me!" Addison protested. "Live dangerously—that's what I say. She's over there near Mrs. Prentice. Blonde in the black dress."

Carew whistled softly. *"Not* Iris Hilder?"

"Uh-huh!" Addison agreed. "The boss-man's secretary. Smart cookie, eh?"

"She's always well-groomed, Max. But tonight she looks . . . really attractive. Younger, somehow."

"I bring 'em out," Addison said complacently. "But believe me, that dame has a calculator where her heart should be. Ten minutes with me, and she knows more about Max Addison and the profit and loss account of the Calco Flying Ambulance Service than I do. I'm afraid I'm not going to like it when she strikes a balance."

Carew chuckled. "You don't have to tell me anything about Iris Hilder's efficiency."

"She's got brains all right. The trouble is we're interested in different kinds of figures. The ones I like wear nylon."

Addison drifted away, and Carew joined Roy Flagg in a quiet corner of the reception room over a parting bourbon that someone had put into their hands. It tasted raw after Scotch, but he drank with Flagg.

"Spot of luck for us, Roy. Your replacement's already on the job."

"So Dr. Prentice told me, Glen. Did he tell you I knew Alden Vaizey back East?"

"Yes. But you've left him a precedent that will be hard to live up to, Roy. Think he can do it?"

"If I told you no, I'd be boasting. As an intern, and that's the way I remember Vaizey, he was good in the surgical service. He could be a good anesthesiologist someday."

"Could?"

Flagg frowned. "If he's interested enough. He can be brilliant at anything when he wants to be. He has that sort of mind. But he likes to play. An anesthesiologist, if he wants to be a good one, has to be *interested*. It's like being a surgeon. You're good. I've seen you carry out surgery that in any big city hospital would have been done only by a specialist in that particular branch of surgery. But you make it look easy. That isn't all ability, or skill. It's being interested in what you're doing. It's application —the fact that you're doing the one thing in life you want to do."

Carew nodded. "I suppose that applies to anything. What makes you think Vaizey isn't really interested in anesthesiology?"

"Did I say *anesthesiology?* When I knew Vaizey, he was an intern, I was a resident. And you know the resident-intern relationship in a big hospital. It isn't as easygoing as it is here at County. We used to keep them on their toes, haze them most of the time. We'd been treated the same way ourselves. An intern makes mistakes. He's in the process of changing from theory to practice. He's finding that it isn't as cut and dried as the textbooks say. So when they make a mistake, you blast them. Residents outdo one another in sarcasm. You hurt the interns' pride. That way, they never forget a mistake, or make it again. They're the better for it."

"That's the usual picture."

"We balled out all the interns in the surgical service. But good! All *except* Alden Vaizey. Whatever he did, he did precisely the right way. Textbook—the right way. But as disinterestedly as though he didn't give a damn. That was okay in general surgery. But anesthesiology is different. It's more personal. Each patient has his own individual reaction to anesthesia, psychologically as well as physically. A good anesthesiologist has to *understand* his patient, know his allergies, his reactions, his physical weaknesses. Has to know the surgeon and how *he* works. Has to be able to balance the surgical need against the patient's strength and the patient's tolerance to anesthesia. That ability, or gift, or what-have-you, isn't in the textbooks. It's in yourself."

"You don't think Vaizey has it?" Carew persisted.

"It has to be the one thing you want to do. That's a start. If you're *interested* enough, maybe the rest will come. I'm sure that Carter could do it. Vaizey—? You answer that, Glen. I can't." He shook hands. "Kris is looking for me. This is it. Thanks for everything, Glen."

36

"Good luck!" Carew called after him. His eyes sought Kathie, and found her coming toward him.

The excitement of the departure caught them up, and Glen Carew thought of the new resident again only briefly as the reception began to break up. He shouldn't have asked Roy Flagg about Alden Vaizey. He should judge the new man on his work at County, and on that alone.

Too many people were going to have preconceived opinions about Alden Vaizey once the details of his uncontested appointment leaked out. And they would leak out. Too many people would be looking for faults in him. Even the usually unbiased Dr. Prentice was starting out with a resentment that, if analyzed, should rightly be for Alden Vaizey's uncle. And in justice to the new resident, Carew was determined not to make the same mistake.

Bill Randall left the reception with Valerie Cassidy soon after the newly married couple drove off. He had been looking forward to driving Valerie back to her small apartment, and her anxiety was beginning to irritate him. He was sure that Valerie was being unnecessarily concerned about her friend, and the sooner he proved that to her, the sooner she would relax.

The apartment house had three floors reached by winding stairs, and the two girls lived on the third. The building was new, born of the rapid growth of the town, and mostly served bachelor girls in small two-room apartments, each with maid service, identical furnishings, the same cooking and breakfast alcove off the same living rooms.

He kissed her on the second-floor landing in the light of the all-night neons flashing along distant Humboldt Avenue, but found her still worried and unresponsive.

"You'll see, honey," he said, taking her hand. "We'll find Carol at home, waiting for you to tell her all about tonight."

But Carol's apartment was dark and silent. Valerie rang the bell and listened. She shook her head. "I knew she wouldn't be here."

"Woman's intuition?"

"Don't laugh at me, Bill," she pleaded.

37

He sobered at the distress in her eyes. "I'm sorry, kid! Okay. We'll start looking. You got a phone?"

"Sure."

"I'll call Ed Fisher, at the Sheriff's Office."

She stopped with her key in the lock. "I don't want to make any trouble. I mean, if the police come here asking questions . . . the other girls will talk."

"Don't worry, Ed's a friend of mine. I operated on him once when someone put a bullet into him. I'll just ask Ed to make some discreet inquiries, and call us back. Unofficially. Ed knows everything that happens in this town, and that will keep it just among the three of us. Okay?"

She considered that as she switched on the light and closed the door behind them. She nodded then, but worry still showed in her troubled green eyes.

"You're very understanding, Bill. I've spoiled your night."

"Not yet you haven't!" He winked mischievously. "The night's still young. And if we find your friend . . ."

He turned her around and kissed her, a slow, experienced kiss.

"Umm!" she said, when she caught her breath.

"Which means?"

"We'll see!" she answered breathlessly, disengaging herself. "In the meantime . . . maybe I should get you some coffee."

"What makes you think it's coffee I need?" he asked, pulling her to him again.

"Bill! Don't—"

His lips at the smooth contour where her throat and shoulder merged made her tingle. Earlier, when she had accepted the date, she had believed he'd be reasonably easy to control. Now, she wasn't so sure. She wasn't even sure that she'd *want* to control him if . . .

She slipped away, her hands going up to her hair with an unconsciously feminine gesture. "You were going to call your friend Ed Fisher. Remember?"

"Eh? Oh sure!"

"The phone's on the table near the window. I'll make the coffee." She walked into the alcove away from him.

Randall grinned. "I still think we'll find she's okay.

38

Maybe she got called out of town unexpectedly. Didn't you say she came from Illinois?"

"She wouldn't go that far away without telling me. Or leaving a message. And she hasn't taken any clothes. I checked this morning when the girl was cleaning the apartment. How do you like your coffee?"

"Laced," he said. "On a night like this."

"I don't have any bromide, but there's some phenobarb Carol gave me—"

"Hey!" he said. "I don't need sedation!"

"That's a matter of opinion!" she told him.

She liked the way he laughed. "If it wasn't for Carol," she thought. But her worry came back as she listened to him talking to Ed Fisher. It was like a black cloud of depression that she couldn't shake off. She brought in the coffee as Bill Randall hung up.

"I tell you, honey, you're worrying over nothing. Ed hasn't heard a thing. But he said he'll check—and call back as quickly as he can."

She found a fifth of rye and added a little to the coffee. Perhaps the whisky would make her feel better. . . .

"County residence was never like this," he said, sitting down on the divan. He sniffed appreciatively at his coffee. "Or County coffee."

"Or County nurses?"

"That might take further investigation," he said judicially. "Deeper analysis. . . ."

"Like this?"

This time *she* kissed him. She wasn't sure if she had been prompted by the warmth of the whisky in her coffee, or if it was because she felt grateful to him for trying to find out about her friend, Carol. Or maybe this warm feeling stirring inside her even meant that she was falling in love. Only it couldn't be that. People didn't fall in love on their first date.

"So what the heck?" she thought. "I just want him to kiss me."

Bill Randall became aware that the phone was ringing. He stroked the girl's flushed face and released her gently.

"You've got me like a Roman candle that's just started to smolder."

39

"Don't pretend you don't *like* feeling Roman candlish," she said drowsily. She sat up from where he had pulled her across his lap into his arms after her kiss.

He reached for the phone. "With you," he said, "*how* I like it!" He spoke into the mouthpiece. "Huh? Ed? No, not you. . . . Okay, did you learn anything?"

"What is it, Bill?" she asked sharply, watching his expression again as he listened to the voice coming thinly over the phone. He frowned her into silence. Briefly, she had seen compassion in his eyes, but now his face was a doctor's face. A serious mask. Void of all personal expression suddenly. He stood up as though to hear better.

"Bill!" she whispered. "Bill—what is it?"

The warmth was gone from her. She felt cold, listening to his emotionless voice as he answered. There was no gaiety, no mischief in Bill Randall's eyes now. They were cold and angry.

"Yes, Ed," he said. "I know it is." Finally, "Thanks Ed. I appreciate what you've done."

"What is it?" she cried. "Bill . . . please!"

He put the phone back on its cradle slowly.

"Bill—?"

"Did you know she was pregnant, Val?" he asked sternly. "Is that why you were so worried?"

She stared at him, white-faced. Her lips trembled. He put an arm around her to steady her.

"I didn't *know*. She never said anything. I just *thought* she was. I heard her getting sick—" Her voice broke. "Bill—tell me!"

The night that had started out so well, that only a few moments ago had been full of exciting promise, had suddenly become grim.

"The bastard!" he thought, his mind seeking the unknown person responsible for what he had just heard. Every now and then they got them at County. They did something to themselves. But this was different—this was *murder!* "I'd like to get my hands on him, or her . . ." he thought viciously.

"Bill!" she pleaded. "Bill, she isn't—?"

He said slowly, "Carol Vincent died two hours ago in County Hospital, from hemorrhage following an attempted abortion."

He held her, feeling her first sobs against his shoulder. Consoling her, he felt sexless. Over her bowed head, through the window of the apartment he watched the lights of Calco County Hospital brooding over the town from where it stood on high ground above the river.

Bill Randall sat very still, holding the girl, waiting for his anger to fade . . . for her grief to subside.

From where he sat in his car outside the nurses' residence, Glen Carew could see the town below him, pinpointed by familiar lights. The neons along Humboldt flashed red, green, and yellow. The street lights crossed at right angles and ran in straight lines. A few late cars coming down the winding road from the mountains to the east reached headlight beams up high as the cars crossed a crest, steadied, and floated down toward the town.

He said without looking at the girl beside him, "I want to thank you for tonight, Kathie. You made it perfect."

A car door slammed over at the garages, and two interns walked across the drive. Their low voices came to them.

"Can't say I go for the Nordic type myself, but Kristina was really something tonight."

"Glowing like an ember. Old Flagg could give himself a coronary, just—Hey! D'you suppose Kris would be a virgin?"

"Huh? In this day and age? Anyway, Flagg's a damned skillful doctor."

"And the loss of a hymen is never fatal, they tell me. Say, I once saw Gregson operate on an imperforate hymen down in L.A. A complete closure, and damned serious. He let a crowd of students observe from the gallery. Told us it might be the only time we'd ever get to see one. . . ."

The voices, the laughter, the crisp sound of shoes on gravel faded.

"Interns!" Kathie Forrest muttered.

Carew smiled in the darkness. "We were all interns, students, student nurses once. You grow out of it, if you survive."

But the voices had broken something that had been

41

growing between them, something born of their closeness of sitting here. . . .

"And your profession takes you," Kathie said softly. "What is there then?"

Carew faced her. "A different kind of satisfaction."

She was tempted to speak of loneliness. But it wasn't that. There was never time to be lonely.

She laughed. "And our Director of Nurses has me scheduled for a little of that satisfaction, beginning at seven. Good night, Glen—"

"Don't go yet." His hand stopped her. She stilled at the touch, trembling.

"Don't spoil it, Glen," she thought. "Please!"

Her voice was calm. "Yes?"

"I don't know when I've enjoyed a night so much, Kathie—not in a long time. Not since—"

She said gently, "Not since a girl you were in love with died?"

"That's right. I thought I'd forgotten how to enjoy myself. But something was different tonight. It was because I was with you. I'm . . . very fond of you, Kathie. . . ." He said it awkwardly.

"That isn't the way I feel about you, Glen," Kathie Forrest thought bitterly. "Fondness isn't love."

She turned with his hands on her shoulder, wanting to resist a pressure that was gentle but compelling. He was going to kiss her, she knew.

I've loved you for so long, Glen, she thought. But with you it's only companionship. It's a night you've enjoyed. I'm glad you did enjoy it. You've needed that for a long time.

But that wasn't love. And how did you compete with a girl who was dead but still held a man? That sort of love was compulsive, could become an obsession. . . .

"I'm flattered, Glen," she said.

He looked at her doubtfully. "It wasn't meant as flattery, Kathie. I never thought I'd need to explain the way I felt about a woman again. You know the story. I *was* in love. We were going to marry. She died. That's the essence of it. But do bald words ever explain a thing like that? They can't explain what we shared. The things I

42

can't forget. The way it was with us. Can I help it if I'm a one-woman man? Would you have me different?"

"No," she said in a low voice.

"But the way I feel toward you is something very special, Kathie. Did you realize tonight was different for us?"

She smiled faintly in the darkness. "Because tonight is the first time we've . . . been out together? Apart from mercy flights?"

He nodded. "Perhaps. Would you say that was why tonight, for the first time, I found myself wishing that I'd met *you* down in L.A. a long time ago? Before I . . . fell in love with someone else?"

She trembled. Her heartbeat was quickening, and she could feel warmth in her face. It was *like* an avowal of love. But could she be satisfied with that?

She said, "Perhaps."

He shook his head. "No, I don't think so, Kathie. I don't think it's just because we went out together as invited guests to a wedding reception. Do you know what I think it is?"

"Maybe it's physical," she said with forced lightness.

"I'm afraid it's more than that."

You're *afraid?* she thought. Don't you want to lose a dream, a memory, a dead woman?

She started to move away, saying with a bitterness that she couldn't hide, *"Good night,* Glen."

But he would not release her. His head was bending, his hands moved beneath her shoulders, molding her to him as he kissed her. He felt withdrawal, then warmth. Her lips clung, warm, trembling. Woman's lips, rousing desire in him.

"I'm afraid I'm falling in love with you, Kathie," he said thickly.

She pulled away from him with unexpected strength. She opened the door and slipped out.

"You're *afraid—!"*

He had never heard her voice bitter or angry like that before. He watched her walking quickly toward the nurses' residence. She ran up the entrance steps. She was gone.

Glen Carew jabbed at the starter. He parked the car in

its garage and went moodily up to his own quarters. A light burned beneath the adjoining door and he could hear movement in there. Dr. Lindemann was up late tonight. Perhaps there'd been another emergency.

He found his key, and was opening the door when he heard the sharp sound of something falling. He waited. Lindemann's movements sounded heavy, labored. Carew could hear him mumbling to himself in German, the words guttural and incoherent.

Carew forgot his own need to be alone. He tapped on the door. "Carl, are you okay in there?"

He listened, frowning, to the heavy, uncertain footsteps approaching. Then Lindemann pulled the door open and stood there, gaping.

"Dr. Carew . . . I am not on call."

"Of course not, Carl. I heard something fall. I thought you might be ill." Carew's serious face broke into a smile. Carl Lindemann wasn't ill—he was drunk. So drunk that he was having difficulty in standing, even with the door for support. The smell of whisky on his breath enveloped Carew as he leaned forward.

"Drunk, Doctor. But sick too. Sick in mind."

Carew thought he had never known Lindemann to be drunk before. Or even to drink. He looked past Lindemann at the bourbon bottle on the small desk, and an overturned glass.

"That doesn't sound like you, Carl."

"No? Perhaps not. You will come in. There is a little left in the bottle. I went to sleep at the desk. . . . Please come in." He stood aside, controlling his equilibrium with visible effort.

Carew came in and closed the door. "Something upset you, Carl? Not bad news?"

Lindemann blinked at him. "It was just tonight. Just . . . Emergency. I came back here hours ago, but I could not sleep. So . . ."

Carew accepted the glass Lindemann filled. He added water.

"It was the girl."

Carew's mind checked. "What girl?"

"She was brought here in collapse. Uterine hemorrhage."

Carew put his drink down. It seemed to be a night for seeing people as strangers. Kathie bitter, angry without reason . . . now the phlegmatic Dr. Carl Lindemann distraught, his face working as though he was about to cry. He brought a chair. He sat Lindemann down.

"We all have our difficult nights, Carl. Uterine hemorrhage isn't all that bad. Transfusion—"

Lindemann shook his head. "She refused transfusion. I was not there. I was in the Recovery Room. Ward, the intern, called me. When I got there, she was dead. So young . . . a lovely girl."

"Dead?"

Lindemann nodded.

"Hemorrhage? Following abortion?"

"Ward thought so. When she refused the transfusion, he started a saline drip through an ankle cutdown. He introduced ergot to contract the uterus."

Carew nodded, frowning. "It sometimes works." He looked at Lindemann. "Ward should have had a resident with him."

"A resident took over," Lindemann said. He drank his whisky and water in straight swallows, as though he was drinking beer. He poured another. "Dr. Vaizey!"

"Go on."

"You know what an oxytocic drug can do to an ectopic pregnancy, Dr. Carew? Of course you do! The contractions start. It is like labor. The tubal pregnancy bursts the tube. It ruptures into the abdominal cavity."

"My God!" Carew said. "Was Vaizey there when Ward gave the ergot?"

"He came later. The girl was dying. Almost comatose."

"He diagnosed an ectopic pregnancy? Ruptured?"

Lindemann shook his head heavily. He was having difficulty in concentrating suddenly. His thoughts were becoming incoherent.

"Pretty," he said. "A dark-haired girl. Not a blemish on her."

"Lindemann!" Carew said sharply. "What about Ward?"

"I suspended his duties for the time being. Until you can check, of course. Until Dr. Prentice decides what is to be done."

"You're sure it was a tubal pregnancy, an ectopic?"

45

Carew was seeing the trouble that lay ahead—for Ward, for the hospital. "Dr. Vaizey may not have had much experience with ectopic pregnancy. It doesn't happen that frequently."

Lindemann shook his head. "Abortion—criminal abortion, they thought. And maybe, yes, that too. Someone ignorant, who thought it an uncomplicated pregnancy. Maybe . . . yes. I hope so. I hope it was done before Ward gave her . . ." His head drooped sleepily.

"Lindemann!"

He looked up again. "Vaizey was gone. Ward came back with me. He would have transfused her after the ergot. But Dr. Vaizey would not allow it against the girl's will. There could not have been much time to decide. No. . . ."

"Who diagnosed the ectopic pregnancy?"

"There was a palpable mass lower than it should have been in the abdomen. I could feel a hematoma, a mass. Left quadrant."

"You diagnosed it?"

"After she was dead—yes. In the morning the P.M. will prove or disprove that. Such a shame. Such a waste of womanhood. Poor Ward. . . ." He was no longer sure whether it was the girl he was sorry for or Ward. He wanted to go to sleep.

"What the hell did Vaizey *do?*" Carew demanded.

"I was not there. Miss Flint said he made an examination—gloved hand. After he sent Ward away, he just stood. She said at the end he ordered her to start a transfusion. Ward had the blood waiting. She started to set it up, but the girls was *in extremis*. Tomorrow at the post-mortem, Dr. Maitland . . ." His head drooped and he snored. The snore wakened him, he looked around foolishly. "Not tomorrow—today. . . ."

Carew got him into bed. He pulled off his shoes and covered him. Then he went back to his own rooms to think about what lay ahead.

The thoughts of Kathie Forrest were long gone.

46

CHAPTER FOUR

"SAY, is this the girl who died last night in Emergency?" the intern from Gynecology asked. "Hemorrhage? I thought that didn't happen any more."

"There's always the exception," remarked one of the off-duty interns who had gathered to watch the autopsy.

"Yeah, but in this modern age of surgery, with transfusion, antibiotics to control infection, how'd it happen?"

"I heard it was an ectopic, and some crumb gave her an oxytocic."

Someone nudged the talkative intern, and he fell silent as Dan Ward and Jim Keaton came in together.

Ward's expression was bleak. He looked at the body stretched out nude on the concave-surfaced autopsy table and turned away, sickened. Except for her pallor and the transparency of her skin from blood loss, she could have been sleeping under sedation or hypnosis.

"My God," Keaton said. "That dame sure was pretty. I didn't realize last night she'd look like that. Like a marble sculpture, eh? No wonder some guy—"

"Shut up!" Ward said.

Keaton looked at him in surprise. "I only meant—"

"Just don't talk about her!"

"Okay, okay!" Keaton said. Sympathy supplanted indignation, and he moved back nearer the wall. "Over

47

here, Dan, he said gruffly. "We can *hear*. Let the ghouls watch."

The door of the autopsy room opened and County's Pathology chief, Dr. Maitland, came in, followed by a group of the hospital staff. The interns quieted when they saw the Medical Superintendent, Dr. Stanley Prentice, walking in with Glen Carew, followed by Dr. Lindemann and Dr. Lindsay, who was chief of Obstetrics and Gynecology.

There were a lot of curious glances at the new resident, who came in last talking in a low voice to Bill Randall. Alden Vaizey's eyes found Ward over against the wall, and he nodded.

Keaton appraised Ward's angry glare in response. "I don't blame you for disliking the guy, Dan," he whispered. "But—"

"I'd like to take that crumb, and—"

"Shh!" Keaton whispered. "Cut it out, Dan! You're in enough trouble now! After all, what did he *do* last night?"

"Nothing! That's what he did! He let her die."

"Dan!" Keaton hissed. "Shut up! You can't say things like that. Not unless you can prove them. What could he have done?"

"The transfusion was ready!"

"She'd refused it. You told me that yourself."

Ward fell silent, scowling. Always when he thought about last night, he came back to that. Maybe if he'd just put a screen, and changed the bottle on the other side of it without her knowledge—? Maybe she'd be alive, instead of lying here on a slab?

Maitland was putting on a heavy rubber apron. The morgue orderly pushed the instrument table closer and glanced at the body disinterestedly before he looked around the group of faces.

"All right, gentlemen," Maitland said quietly. "Move back a little, please. I don't want someone jogging my elbow and making me cut myself. My sensory perceptions still allow *me* to feel pain."

"The ghoul!" Ward hissed.

"He's a good pathologist," Keaton said. "And he'll find out what happened to her. Snap out of it, Dan. Try to

48

forget she was your patient. If she'd been someone else's admission, this'd be just another autopsy."

"It isn't easy to forget she *was* my patient."

"Shh!"

Maitland was looking at Dr. Prentice. He prepared to start. "A complete autopsy, Doctor?"

"I want to know all about her, as well as the cause of death." His expression was formidable. "*All* about her, Dr. Maitland."

"That will take some time. I'll start with the heart."

He worked quickly. Ward watched the first incision, fascinated, before he started to feel sick. He closed his eyes then, and leaned back against the wall.

"Hey!" Keaton whispered. "What's up? *Christ!* You weren't sick at your first anatomy-class dissection! What's got into you?"

"I'm . . . all right," Ward said thickly.

"Sit down! Just slide down the wall and bend your head."

"No. I'm all right." He opened his eyes. He looked as pale as the cadaver that Maitland was cutting.

Maitland cut quickly, making a V-shaped incision from the shoulders to the lower edge of the breastbone.

"You wouldn't think she'd have any blood left," one of the interns whispered.

Blood was draining away from the concave surface of the table, gathering sluggishly into troughs that lined the table. Maitland removed the incised segment of breast-plate. He reached for the bloodied heart. . . .

Bill Randall was staring at the dissected body, seeing in it the girl who had been Valerie's friend—as the girl she must have been. Valerie had talked a lot about Carol Vincent last night. And he had let her talk until she grew tired, pouring whisky at intervals for her, because that was the only thing having sedative qualities that he could reach without moving.

He had soothed her, taken off her shoes. And when she had gone to sleep eventually, he had risen tired and cramped from where he had sat beside her on the divan. He had found covers in the bedroom and made her comfortable.

Randall sighed, remembering how he had kissed the

49

sleeping girl lightly before he left, closing the door securely behind him.

"She could still be sleeping," he thought, seeing a mental picture of her as she had looked when he was leaving.

She hadn't looked as pretty or as sophisticated then. With her make-up streaked by tears, her eyes puffed, she had looked like a sad little girl, lost and alone.

He brought himself back to the present. Maitland had clamped off the vessels to the heart and now he was opening the ventricles under water, checking for the remote possibility of an air embolism introduced when Ward had made the ankle cutdown. No air bubbles rose. Blood from the heart's chambers stained the water. That was all.

"Healthy young heart," Maitland said. "No sign of anything there to worry us."

He began cutting again. Randall looked up and saw Vaizey's face. It was pale, but Vaizey was watching calmly.

He caught Randall's glance and said quickly, "Do you have much of this sort of thing in Calco? I mean abortion?"

Randall frowned. "Sometimes they do things to themselves. It's about the same in Calco as any other place. But we haven't had an abortionist here before. I'd like to get my hands on him, or her. Now, I suppose, we'll have a rash of this kind of thing until he's caught. I hope it's soon!"

"We don't know that we do have one," Vaizey said. "I've heard it's hard to prove. At law, I mean."

"*I'm* satisfied we have one," Randall said.

"Even before the autopsy is completed?" Vaizey said. "Have you made an examination of the body yourself, Doctor?"

Randall glanced at Glen Carew and saw his steady eyes watching him also.

He said, "I wasn't here last night, Doctor. This is the first time I've seen her, dead or alive."

Carew said, "What's all this about, Bill?"

"She was a friend of the girl I was with last night. You met Val Cassidy. Val was worried about her. When I took her back to her apartment, she talked about this girl quite a lot. She suspected that she was pregnant and had had something done about it. The night before last Carol Vincent didn't come back to her apartment. She stayed out all night. And all yesterday. Val rents the next apartment."

"The chest organs are all perfectly healthy," Maitland's voice interposed. "Nothing there that we could diagnose as a primary condition that could cause death."

Vaizey said in a low voice, looking at Randall, "If your friend knows her that well, she should know the name of the man responsible for the pregnancy."

"And that could lead us to whoever did this," Carew said. "If it's a criminal abortion we can put the bastard where he belongs. For a long time."

Randall had never seen Carew's eyes as angry, but the same deep anger had stirred in himself last night, when Ed Fisher told him.

He shook his head. "Val didn't know she had a lover. Or where she was yesterday and the night before—" He broke off. "Is something the matter, Dr. Vaizey?"

Vaizey was wiping his forehead with a handkerchief. His laugh was a little forced. "It's hot in here, Doctor. That's all. I've seen an autopsy before."

Maitland was preparing to open the abdomen. There was a stir of interest among the doctors and interns. The answer to the girl's death would be here, they knew.

Maitland said calmly, "Dr. Lindemann examined the body last night. He diagnosed an ectopic pregnancy rupture with resultant hemorrhage into the abdomen as the primary cause of death. Well, we'll soon know."

Heads turned at a startled sound over near the wall. Ward was walking blindly toward the door.

Carew said quickly, "Carl, you didn't tell Ward about your diagnosis last night?"

"No, I didn't," Lindemann said. His brown eyes watched Ward groping for the door. "I had to be sure. I could not tell him *that* last night and be sure. I just canceled his duties until the autopsy."

"The girl refused a transfusion," Vaizey said. "It was against her religious beliefs. There are sects like that. If you blamed Ward for not transfusing, you would have to blame me also."

Keaton's voice said sharply, "Dan, wait! I'm coming

51

with you." He was walking over to Ward, as Maitland spoke. Absorbed by his work, Maitland hadn't noticed anything else.

"And Dr. Lindemann was right," Maitland's voice said. "There *was* an ectopic pregnancy. The tube is ruptured. The embryo has passed through the wall of the Fallopian tube into the abdomen—I would say under considerable pressure, as though by spasm, or contraction. This is interesting, Dr. Lindsay. The tube usually ruptures at about the sixth week, but this gestation is smaller, has aborted earlier."

"God!"

Ward had stumbled out with the word.

Maitland looked toward the door, surprised. "Don't tell me," he said, "interns still have weak stomachs?" He bent again, extracting the gestation.

The group of doctors around Dr. Lindsay moved in closer.

"Diagnosis ruptured tubal gestation," Lindsay said. "Cause of death parenchymatous hemorrhage? That it, Maitland?"

"That could be the essence of my report," Maitland said. "Let's have a look at the uterus."

Watching him dissect the uterus, Carew said, "Are you satisfied the rupture was caused naturally, Doctor? You mentioned spasm or contractions. The gestation looks too small to cause the rupture without *severe* contractions."

Maitland frowned. "That's right. Very severe contractions."

"Such as could be caused by the administration of ergot, given to contract the uterus in the normal procedure of trying to correct a uterine hemorrhage?" Dr. Prentice asked.

Maitland looked worried. "Dr. Lindsay?"

Lindsay frowned. "It *could.*"

"I'll have to run tests," Maitland said, "before I could give one injection of ergot as the cause of contractions strong enough to create the condition that's happened here." He shook his head. "It would have had to be a massive dose."

"It was three cc.'s," Carew said. "I checked."

Lindsay shook his head. "At full pregnancy, a normal pregnancy, that would cause long contractions."

"This isn't normal, or full time," Carew said, thinking of Ward walking blindly outside. "Gentlemen, I don't believe we're on the right track."

Prentice said sharply, "Can you suggest something else?"

"Why not? It's been in all our minds."

Prentice said, "I shouldn't have said *suggest*. *Prove* is the word we need. Well, Doctor?"

"The whole thing is unfortunate, but do you think it's wise to twist it into something worse that we can't prove?" Vaizey asked, a faint smile twisting his lips.

"I think you should explain that, Dr. Vaizey," Carew said.

Vaizey shrugged. "I just meant that here we have the case of an intern who has given an intravenous injection of an oxytocic drug to contract a uterus to control hemorrhage. If the pregnancy had been normal, that's the way it should have acted. But the intern missed the diagnosis of an ectopic pregnancy. The symptoms indicated abortion, and there was uterine hemorrhage. It was an emergency, and he took emergency steps to relieve it. He made a mistake—one almost any of us could make under the same circumstances. It isn't going to ruin his career. And in the final analysis, what he did made little difference to the girl. That's why I say, should we look for an alternative? Ward will be the better doctor for this little slip."

"Nobody gets whitewashed here. *Or* accused, until we're sure," Prentice said sternly.

"You were there," Randall said. "Did *you* know it was ectopic?"

"I accepted Ward's diagnosis provisionally—until I made my own examination."

"And then?" Carew said, watching him.

Vaizey glanced around the watching faces. They were hostile with the exception of Carew's.

"I examined her, Dr. Carew. I found a palpable mass, signs of internal hemorrhage as well as the uterine hemorrhage that Ward had thought the only trouble. The examination indicated immediate surgery for a ruptured tubal pregnancy on the left side. But she could not survive

53

surgery without preliminary transfusion. I had to decide whether to go against her wishes and transfuse her. She was in shock, drifting into coma and collapse. I believed she'd die without transfusion. The prognosis was bad. Miss Flint will tell you that I had her prepare to transfuse whole blood. I said I'd take the responsibility for that. But the patient was already collapsing. She died as the transfusion began. I believe it was already too late when she was brought into Emergency."

Lindemann said heavily, "When I came in, you had gone. There was no report."

"Ah," Vaizey said. "The Teutonic mind, Doctor! Reports! I was distressed. This girl was my first patient here. How would any of you feel under the same circumstances? I walked outside on the lawns for a few minutes. Then I came back and filled out the death certificate for Dr. Prentice. Right, sir?"

Prentice nodded, frowning. "The report suggested ectopic pregnancy, and asked for a P.M. Essentially, the report was a duplication of Dr. Lindemann's."

Randall said impatiently, "Dr. Carew was about to say something when this angle came up. I'd like to hear what he had to say. But first—after the wedding reception last night I had inquiries made about this girl. She had been missing from her apartment for almost twenty-four hours. I found that she died here two hours earlier. I'd like to know what happened in the time between her leaving the apartment and being brought here in collapse *and* already hemorrhaging—hemorrhaging long before she was given a contracting drug by Ward. I think that's the question we need answered."

Carew finished talking to Maitland in a low voice, and looked up from where he had moved in beside the pathologist.

"I was about to say the same thing. This girl had lost a lot of blood. More than she lost here last night. Or in the phone booth where they found her. In my opinion she had been hemorrhaging for many hours. A gradually increasing hemorrhage that culminated in collapse. Some time during that period, and before she was brought here, the tube ruptured. Long before Dr. Ward gave her ergot. We all know what that means. Abortion."

54

"Self-induced?"

Carew looked for the speaker. Alden Vaizey again. He stifled dislike. Vaizey had a right to question. He was directly concerned.

Carew said, *"Not* self-induced! Dr. Maitland?"

Maitland looked up. "The condition of the coagulum in the abdomen indicates that the hemorrhage began some time ago. I can't say exactly, but it was at least six hours before she was brought here. The uterine hemorrhage probably began much earlier than that. In my opinion an oxytocic drug caused the uterine hemorrhage, and later the tubal gestation rupture. There are indications of the use of pitressin or pitocin. She's been injected, gentlemen, and she didn't do that herself. Ward gave her ergot through an ankle vein. But there are four needle marks in the shoulder muscles. She couldn't give herself a needle there. When I run some tests, I'll be able to name the drug precisely. But someone gave her a pituitary extract drug to cause an abortion. They gave it to her to terminate what they thought an ordinary pregnancy. Someone with medical knowledge, and access to medical supplies."

Prentice rasped, "Someone from here?"

Maitland shook his head. "Why from here?"

Carew said angrily, "Someone with the opportunity to steal the drug and a hypodermic? Someone with enough medical knowledge to use the drug? In Gynecology they inject patients in the shoulder muscles. Whoever gave these needles knew that. Four needles indicate that the abortionist was worried. He was injecting her, and getting contractions, but nothing else was happening. Hemorrhage probably, not a great deal at first. Uterine hemorrhage. He stepped up the needles to four. And he had enough medical knowledge not to exceed that. Or perhaps he was just scared, and wanted to be rid of her by then. He had some medical knowledge, but he was ignorant too."

Vaizey said slowly, "Ignorant? Why do you say—ignorant?"

"Because whoever it was didn't know an ectopic pregnancy when they saw one," Carew said, his face hardening. "So this girl died."

"It need not have been a man," Vaizey said. "It could have been a woman. A nurse maybe?"

"Or an orderly?"

"Or maybe a doctor," an intern said looking around, his young face grim.

"I don't see how it could be a *doctor*," Carew said coldly. "At least, not as I define the term. No experienced doctor would do this—he couldn't! But whoever it is, whether he did it out of ignorance or negligence or drunkenness or Lord knows what—I'd like to see that he gets what's coming to him, if I have to drag him into court myself!"

"You and me both," Randall said grimly. "And I'd help you do it!"

CHAPTER FIVE

CAREW, Maitland, and Lindsay sat on chairs along the wall of Dr. Prentice's office and listened to the cold, impersonal voice of the Medical Examiner asking interminable questions. When the questions were addressed to them personally, they answered. But mostly they smoked and listened to questions that Dr. Markwell, the Medical Examiner, asked a nervous and angry intern, Dan Ward, or a seemingly almost bored resident doctor, Alden Vaizey.

The Medical Examiner was in his late fifties, lean and graying and professionally efficient. His keen mind had been trained to investigate the weaknesses and find the faults in members of his profession.

The office of the Medical Examiner was an extremely efficient and incorruptible organization. It worked closely with the District Attorney's Office whenever there was a possible medical basis for investigation of a death by the District Attorney's Office. They were investigating such a death right now—Carol Vincent, the girl who had died in the Emergency Room at Calco County Hospital.

The Medical Examiner said in his quiet voice, "You are perfectly sure, Dr. Ward, that you injected three cc.'s of ergot into the saline drip through infusion only? No more, Doctor?"

Ward said wearily, "No more." It was not the first time he had answered that question.

"And you gave no other intravenous injection?"

"None."

"And no intramuscular injection of any kind?"

"No." Ward looked around defiantly. "I was giving emergency treatment. I couldn't find a superficial vein quickly. Her pressure was sixty over thirty. I thought a cutdown—"

"You did not use pitressin?"

"No. I did not!"

"Or pitocin?"

"Certainly not."

The Examiner's shrewd eyes turned to Alden Vaizey. "You gave the patient no injections at all, Doctor?"

"None," Vaizey said calmly.

"How long were you with the patient before she died?"

"Five minutes . . . I'm not sure. As I have told you, I was examining the patient, not the clock. Perhaps Miss Flint, the charge nurse on duty, could tell you that."

"She already has." The Examiner was flipping through some notes. "Miss Flint says you were with the patient for ten to fifteen minutes before she died."

"Then I probably was."

"You did not decide to inject her, as supplementary therapy to the ergot that Dr. Ward had already administered?"

"I did not."

"You were in doubt as to the legality of giving the patient a transfusion of whole blood against her wishes?"

Vaizey glanced around at the other doctors. "Yes. To me, it was a hard decision to make. I did not think she could survive without transfusion. But I knew that to give a blood transfusion against a person's religious principles can lead to irreparable harm. It can create . . . distress . . . psychological disturbance."

"I quite agree," the Examiner said mildly. "It can also create a law suit against the hospital and the doctor concerned. Yet, ultimately, you did decide to transfuse the patient. Why?"

Vaizey glanced at Ward's pale, set face, and looked away. "At first I was considering the emergency in the

58

light of Dr. Ward's diagnosis. When I made my own examination, I suspected an ectopic pregnancy in the left Fallopian tube. It had already ruptured into the abdomen, and the indications were for immediate surgery."

"You therefore commenced the transfusion of whole blood at once?"

"Not . . . at once. I had to make my decision first."

"In the meantime, the patient's pressure was falling rapidly?"

"It was falling. Yes."

"She had already been matched and cross-matched for her blood type on Dr. Ward's instructions?"

"Yes."

"And the flask of whole blood was ready to set up?"

"Yes."

"Was she still protesting that she did not want to be transfused?"

Vaizey wet his lips, and turned to County's Medical Superintendent. "Dr. Prentice, I must protest against being treated as though *I* were under suspicion by Dr. Markham. Miss Flint was present all the time I was with the patient. She can tell him I gave no oxytocic drug. That I did not even ask for a hypodermic. She—"

Dr. Prentice glared disapprovingly. "The question was whether the patient protested to you that she would not allow transfusion. I see no reason why you should not answer that, Dr. Vaizey."

Alden Vaizey waved an impatient hand. "I was referring to this whole matter of questioning, not one specific question. However, if Dr. Markham will repeat the question—?"

"The name," the Medical Examiner said gently, "is Markwell. M-a-r-k-w-e-l-l. I hope you are not confusing me with a fictional detective named Markham. However, if after preliminary inquiries here, the Medical Examiner's Office should decide there was criminal intent in this case and should refer it to the District Attorney's Office, I'm sure you'll learn a lot more about detectives and severe questioning. Dr. Vaizey, I merely asked you, did the patient protest to you against transfusion?"

"I heard her telling Dr. Ward—"

"Did she protest to *you?*"

59

"No."

"Was she able to protest to you at the time you made your decision and ordered Miss Flint to begin the transfusion of whole blood?"

"She was lapsing into coma."

"Was she actually unconscious when you ordered the transfusion?"

"I . . . couldn't be sure."

"Did you check to see whether she was in a state of coma then?"

"Not then. Miss Flint started to change the flasks. I think I watched Miss Flint. I'm not sure. When I looked at the patient, she was *in extremis.*"

"There was a return of consciousness at the last?"

"Yes."

"Was she able to speak?"

"Not . . . coherently."

"I see. Dr. Vaizey, I have a statement here from Dr. Ward in which he spoke to the patient, tried to question her. A statement made by a dying patient to an attending physician before death is admissible at law as evidence, provided the patient knows that death is imminent. Unfortunately, Dr. Ward obtained no useful answers to his questions. Nothing concrete. She said she was frightened, that she knew she was about to die. She said, I quote: 'It wasn't a baby. Not yet it wasn't. And *he* said he'd help me. He said there'd be no trouble, no pain.' " Dr. Markwell laid his notes down and looked at Vaizey. "Enough to indicate there had been a criminal abortion performed by a man, wouldn't you say, Doctor? Is something the matter?"

"It's just . . . all this." Alden Vaizey was fumbling with a handkerchief. He mopped his forehead. Sweat had beaded there suddenly. He went pale. "I find it . . . distressing!"

"It is distressing for everyone concerned. You say she did speak, but she was not very coherent? Doctor, I don't have to tell you how important it is that you should add whatever you can to Dr. Ward's statement of what she told him. A doctor usually remembers the words of a dying patient. *What did she say?*"

"Miss Flint was changing the flasks—"

60

"I have Miss Flint's statement of what *she* heard, Doctor. Now I want *yours*. You were closer. You bent over the patient. What did you hear?"

They were all watching Vaizey. Carew glanced around the circle of faces and felt sympathy for the new resident. He had never seen his colleagues' faces as bleak.

"I have to tell you the exact words?"

"There's no authority vested in me that can force you to speak, Doctor," Markwell said dryly. "But if anything that could be considered vital to this informal inquiry was withheld—then I would not be able to advise the Medical Examiner's Office that I was satisfied. The matter would go automatically to the District Attorney."

Vaizey regained control. "As near as I can remember, she said . . ."

"Go on, Doctor."

"She said, 'I didn't . . . mean it!' Then, she . . . she just cried out, 'Oh God!' "

"No names? No indication of the name of the person who . . . helped her?"

Vaizey said in a low voice, "Nothing."

The Medical Examiner closed his notes. "That agrees with Miss Flint's statement, Doctor. It is a pity that some responsible person did not try to obtain more information from her."

"I was only interested in trying to save her life," Vaizey said, white-faced.

"I tried!" Ward said. "I was questioning her when Dr. Vaizey came in. He stopped me—!"

"That's nonsense," Vaizey said.

Dr. Markwell frowned. "Stopped you? Did Dr. Vaizey order you to stop questioning the girl?"

"Well . . ."

"Dr. Ward?"

"Not in so many words . . ."

"I want you to explain that."

"Well, Dr. Vaizey just spoke my name. *'Dr. Ward!'* Sharply, like that. I stopped talking to the patient at once because I thought he wanted to start the transfusion."

"Dr. Vaizey did not order you to stop questioning the girl?"

"Well—no!"

"Then you should not have suggested that he did." He held up a hand as Ward started an indignant protest. "Sit down, please, Dr. Ward. Dr. Vaizey, one more question."

Vaizey said with a new respect in his voice, "Yes, sir?"

"Did the thought of a pressure transfusion occur to you?"

"Yes, it did. But the normal set was already there, as ordered by Dr. Ward. It was my intention to change to a pressure transfusion as soon as possible."

"You considered the use of the set already there an intermediate emergency step?"

"Yes, I did."

"A little belatedly, Dr. Vaizey."

"I protest against—" Vaizey was on his feet, color coming back into his face.

The Medical Examiner waved him down testily. "Later, Doctor! Later! I'm quite prepared to listen to any criticism, or it can be submitted to the Medical Examiner's Office—but right now we're trying to get a clear picture of what happened. Facts are more important than complaints. I want *facts*. A clear clinical picture of what happened to that girl."

Prentice said, "We all want that, Dr. Markwell." He glanced at his watch. "And as quickly as possible. We have a hospital to run."

"I'm aware of that, Dr. Prentice. Dr. Lindsay, would you mind telling us some of the general considerations in tubal pregnancy?"

Lindsay frowned. "Immediate operation is indicated in cases of tubal pregnancy as soon as the diagnosis is made. In rare cases discovered late there is spontaneous recovery. But I have never personally encountered one."

"*Very* rare," Markwell said. "Go on, Doctor."

"Immediate surgery is indicated whether the pregnancy has ruptured the tube or not. When it ruptures, many patients experience rapid hemorrhage into the abdominal cavity and present urgent emergencies, as Miss Vincent did. Unless prompt surgery is instituted, they die quickly. Whole blood should be given for shock and hemorrhage *at once,* and transfusion should be sustained during the operation."

Lindsay glanced around. Carew was nodding slowly. Markwell said, "Go on, Doctor."

"The operation itself is relatively simple. A tubal pregnancy is usually lifted from the pelvis quite easily. Blood is aspirated from the peritoneal cavity. Once the tube is reached, bleeding can be controlled by finger compression of the broad ligament. This is usually done until the blood is cleared from the cavity by suction." He shrugged. "It is not difficult surgery. The mesosalpinx—that part of the broad ligament around the Fallopian tube—is clamped and the tube itself cut away. The ovary can usually be preserved intact. Transfixing sutures seal the broad ligament. The abdominal wound is closed without drainage. But that applies to a normal tubal pregnancy—either not yet ruptured, or ruptured within at the most an hour or so. It did not necessarily apply to Miss Vincent's condition."

"Dr. Carew, I believe your experience as a surgeon has involved a number of gynecological cases. Do you agree with what Dr. Lindsay has just said?"

"Yes."

"Dr. Carew—in your opinion, given immediate transfusion and surgery, could Miss Vincent's life have been saved?"

"I thought we were dealing in facts—not opinions?" Vaizey said in a disgusted voice.

Carew frowned, considering. "I can't answer that, Dr. Markwell. It would depend upon her condition, and the volume of blood loss. I've read the report and studied the chart. But only the attending physicians could give a competent opinion on that. I wasn't there."

"Dr. Lindsay?"

"I agree with Dr. Carew. I wasn't there either. It would only be an opinion."

"I'll put it another way. Given a quick transfusion, and surgery, would the prognosis have been better or worse?"

"It could not be worse."

"Would it have been better?"

Lindsay said reluctantly, "Yes."

"Dr. Carew?"

"The possibility of recovery would still depend upon her condition, and blood loss."

"But the prognosis?" Markwell insisted.

"Would be slightly better," Carew agreed.

"Dr. Lindsay, at what stage of tubal pregnancy does the growing gestation normally burst the tube?"

"At from six to eight weeks."

"Do you agree that in this case the embryo was five weeks and no more?"

Lindsay nodded. "Yes."

"Normally, this tube should not have ruptured?"

"No," Lindsay said, grim-faced.

"But if the patient had been given four massive intramuscular injections of a pituitary extract designed to contract the uterus—what then, Dr. Lindsay?"

"The violent contractions could have caused the pregnancy to rupture through the tube into the abdominal cavity."

"With hemorrhage into the cavity?"

"Yes."

"With a secondary complication of uterine hemorrhage?"

"In some cases."

"Please be specific, Doctor," Markwell said tartly. "In this case?"

"In this case. Yes."

"Dr. Lindsay, you have read the laboratory report, and you were present at the autopsy. Do you agree that the indications are that the deceased was given, at some time within the twenty-four hours preceding her death, sufficient quantity of an oxytocic drug, pitressin, to cause the conditions that led to her death?"

"Yes, I do."

"Dr. Carew?"

"Yes."

"Dr. Maitland?"

The pathologist said quietly, "I agree."

The Medical Examiner shuffled his papers. "As an officer of the Medical Examiner's Office," he said, "my job is to investigate when the cause of death is in doubt. Essentially, I concur with your staff, Dr. Prentice. The rupture of a tubal pregnancy through the tube into the abdomen with resultant hemorrhage caused death. But it does not *explain* the death. Death was chemically induced

64

by the injection of an oxytocic drug administered by some person unknown, with the intention of causing a criminal abortion. I shall report to that effect. But I must insist on a thorough check of your oxytocic drugs. Unless the check proves otherwise, there is no indication that any member of your staff was involved." He glanced around at them. "I shall also report that. Of course, you understand the police will want to make their own inquiries?"

"I understand that," Prentice said grimly. "We'll co-operate, of course. But I'm not looking forward to a police investigation."

Smiling, the Medical Examiner seemed less severe. "You're short-staffed, aren't you? Well, I'll try to keep them out of your hair. There's just one more thing before you return to your duties." He looked around at their stern faces, and his own expression became angry. "Whoever the sonofabitch is, he'll do it again! Ward's questions and the answers she gave him suggest it's a man. And men only do these things for what they can get out of it. Money! So he'll do it again with some other unfortunate girl. And since the incidence of tubal pregnancy is only at the ratio of one to four hundred, next time all you'll see of it, if it comes to you, will be someone who asks for curettage after a normal miscarriage. Or maybe a uterine hemorrhage that really is one this time, if he muffs it again. So with anything that looks remotely like the aftermath of a miscarriage—*you look for needle marks! Understand?"*

He listened with satisfaction to the deep growl of assent.

"If a professional abortionist obtained a supply of an oxytocic drug from some hospital, or from some illicit source of supply, you can bet your life he'd get it in quantity while the opportunity was there. So look for unexplained needle marks in the shoulder muscles. That's his trademark. And the next time—*we'll get him!* Right?"

He stood up, listening to their angry agreement. Putting his papers and notes into a brief case, he waited for their voices to subside.

Dr. Prentice watched him, frowning. The Medical Examiner had more to say yet, he was sure of that. He

65

waited anxiously as the Medical Examiner's eyes sought his.

"By the way, Dr. Prentice, while I appreciate the fact that you *are* short-staffed here at County, I shall have to report to my office that the deceased was left to the—ah—discretion of a comparatively inexperienced intern for a very vital twenty minutes when she was first brought into the Emergency Room."

Prentice flushed. "There was a resident present in Emergency." He glared at Vaizey. "Dr. Vaizey had taken over in the absence of Dr. Lindemann, who had been assisting Dr. Carew at an operation upon an earlier emergency admission."

Markwell nodded soothingly. "Nevertheless, I was sent here to gather the facts, and that's one of them. I can't justly censure Dr. Vaizey, who had just arrived at the hospital and should not have been expected to take over the Emergency Room. Neither will I censure Dr. Ward, who lacked the experience to make the necessary swift decision that—ah—even if it might not have saved a life, could have made the prognosis better."

"Are you censuring *me?*" Dr. Prentice demanded, standing up.

"There were remarkably few experienced doctors on the premises—" Markwell began.

"I considered every hospital service to be adequately covered," Prentice protested stiffly. "Our staff here, Dr. Markwell, functions quite differently from many private hospitals. Nearly all of them live right here and are, in effect, on call twenty-four hours a day. One of their colleagues was being married and several of them attended the wedding. But not one of them would have gone off for the afternoon and evening without my assurance that it was all right to do so. I repeat—we were, I believed, adequately covered."

Markwell had held up both hands in a placating gesture. "Doctor—Doctor! I am not censuring you or your staff! Now, will you hear me out, please? I have a plane to catch. Now . . . I intend to recommend that my office advise the Board of this hospital that in the interest of complete efficiency, at least two new residencies must be established here. I suggest a residency in Surgery, and

66

another in either Obstetrics or Gynecology. That's all, gentlemen. So far as my office is concerned, no blame will be attached to this hospital for what has happened. Dr. Vaizey and Dr. Ward are at liberty to return to their normal duties."

He picked up his brief case. "Don't forget to look for unexplained needle marks. I want that man! Good day, gentlemen."

Dr. Prentice waited, fuming, until the door had closed firmly behind him. "Goddamn his hide!" he said with feeling. He glared around the room. "Dr. Vaizey, you are still suspended from duty, despite the Medical Examiner's decision. You are suspended until *I* advise you otherwise."

"But—" Vaizey had paled and risen quickly to his feet.

"That's all, Doctor! The rest of you can go back to your duties. Except Dr. Carew. Glen, I want to talk to you."

"If you want my resignation—?" Vaizey said bitterly.

"If I do, I'll let you know," Prentice said. "But in the meantime, that's all, Doctor!"

For a moment, Carew thought Vaizey was about to resign on the spot, but his lips compressed tightly and he turned away. Carew glanced at the Medical Superintendent and found his face an angry mask. The normally placid Dr. Prentice had taunted the younger man deliberately. He wanted Vaizey to resign. And that wasn't fair!

"If that's what the Board gives me when *they* choose a new resident, it's the last time they'll get the chance to do it," Prentice said as Alden Vaizey's footsteps retreated through the outer office. "In all the years I've been running this hospital, we've never had trouble with the Medical Examiner's Office before. Now here we are with an adverse report going in about us, no matter how Markwell may have sugar-coated it to us in the telling! We're going to have a police investigation. We'll be reported as allowing an inexperienced intern to deal with a major emergency. As having the kind of resident who stands around while a patient dies. We'll be reported as a lot of pleasure-seeking people who run off to enjoy themselves, leaving the hospital short-staffed—!"

"Hold it, Doctor," Carew said, smiling. "Surely it isn't

as bad as that. Markwell said that no blame will be attached to County. He is recommending two new residencies. We can really use those."

"*If* the Board agrees! And *if* the Board can persuade the County to pay the extra few thousand dollars a year the residencies will cost! Why the hell did Flagg have to get married and run off? This place was running like a well-oiled machine until he left."

Carew grinned. "In the natural order of things, men marry. And when they do, they look for better paid jobs, greater security."

"So two Los Angeles medical proselytizers come here ostensibly to help us in a forest fire disaster, and they steal Flagg away from under our noses. And a Board instituted to help this hospital in an advisory capacity interferes and gives us—*Dr. Vaizey!*"

"Aren't you being a bit rough on Vaizey? It wasn't his fault the girl was brought in at that time. Or that her refusal of transfusion complicated things."

"Are you siding with Vaizey?" Prentice demanded.

Glen Carew frowned. "In a way—yes! I think we're inclined to blame Vaizey for everything that happened. I can't say I like him as a person. And I certainly don't agree with the Board's tactics in foisting him on the hospital without your approval. But neither can I blame him for everything that happens because of that."

Dr. Prentice scowled, but a little of his anger had faded. "Is that the way I appear to be acting? The way it looks to you, Glen?"

"Yes, it is! I've never known you to be prejudiced against any staff member before. You've always been fair. But right now you don't appear to me to be acting fairly toward Alden Vaizey. Markwell cleared him, admittedly with a caution. Can we do less than that? Usually we stick to any staff member in trouble. And that's what Vaizey is at this moment. In trouble with everyone, and not quite sure what it's all about."

"I can feel that way about Ward."

"Ward's little more than a student. Vaizey is a resident. A colleague."

Prentice spread his hands in an angry gesture. "Okay!

Okay! So I'm prejudiced. I had it in mind to keep him suspended for a while."

"Hoping he'd resign?"

"Maybe. All right! Yes. Hoping he'd resign and go elsewhere."

Carew lit a cigarette. "I'm as angry as you are about what happened to that girl. But I'm aiming my anger in a different direction. At what happened before she was brought here. I'm going to do something about that, if I can. As for Dr. Vaizey, whether he stays or goes is up to you. He hasn't had much chance to prove his ability yet."

"Ability?"

"As an anesthesiologist. That's his specialty. Remember?"

"Damn it!" Prentice said. "Whose side are you on, Glen? Okay!" He flicked a switch on the intercom. "Miss Hilder, I want Dr. Vaizey called. He should be at the residence. He is to report for duty to Dr. Carew in the surgical service at once. Yes, the order is from me. Thank you, Miss Hilder, that's all." He snapped off the switch. "Let's see if he's any better as an anesthesiologist," he mumbled.

Carew smiled. "That's more like *you*, Dr. Prentice."

CHAPTER SIX

IN VAIZEY'S department store, Bill Randall wended his way slowly along the counters, making minor purchases. Most of the hospital staff shopped at Vaizey's—not out of any sense of loyalty to the Board Chairman, but because Vaizey's was the largest store in town, and you could shop quickly there. By local standards, it was also cheap.

Randall took the elevator to the third floor. He needed a new sports shirt from the men's department, but he might also see Valerie Cassidy. Valerie worked in the credit office located at the back of the men's department. From where he stood now, he could look into the big office over the counter where customers paid their accounts.

He was remembering that he had first met Valerie Cassidy this way, and on impulse had asked her to go with him to Roy Flagg's wedding soon afterward. That was barely two weeks ago, but it seemed a long time ago now. In hospitals, time either dragged when you were weary, or passed so quickly you had to run to keep up. The last two weeks had been a gallop.

"Maybe that's why I haven't called Val," he told himself, although he knew it wasn't true. It had nothing to do with pressure at the hospital.

He found her now, her blonde head bent as she placed a sheaf of papers on another girl's desk. She straightened and then, as though she felt his eyes upon her, she searched the busy store on the other side of the protective counter. Randall knew the moment she saw him, by the way her green eyes widened. He waved the bill in his hand at her casually before he paid the assistant. When he looked back she was seated at her desk again, her hands carefully arranging her dress before she started typing again as though he wasn't there.

Randall grinned crookedly. No doubt he deserved that. He fought an impulse to walk over to the counter and ask to see Miss Cassidy. But the way she was now pretending complete absorbtion in her work decided him that he might be sticking his chin out. "I like her," he thought. "But—"

It was that *but* that troubled him, had kept him from calling her.

It stemmed, he decided as he watched the assistant wrap his parcel, from what they had shared the night Carol Vincent died. If it hadn't been for that . . .

"Thanks." He took the parcel and lost himself in the crowd. At the elevators he looked back briefly to find her blonde head searching for him. He stood for a moment, undecided, a part of him hoping that she'd find him, and was disappointed when she did not. Then he heard quite distinctly the loud clang with which she rapped back the carriage of her typewriter.

He joined the crowd pushing into an elevator. "And that," he thought moodily, "is the end."

It wasn't that she had lost any attraction for him. Frankly, she was terrific. And she *did* like him. He could probably go back right now, kid her a little, and pick it right up where they'd left off that night. He'd suggest a show and supper. Drive her home around the block to 72 Harker. If she had been responsive then, she would be more responsive now. Only . . .

Bill Randall frowned as he got out of the elevator at street level. That night he had held Valerie Cassidy in his arms like a child. He had stilled her sobs, had watched her fall asleep. That was what made it different. Except for that one time when he had been in love, it was a game you played. It should never be allowed to become anything else. It was a game in which you had successes,

71

or if you made a mistake and were disappointed, you cut your losses and parted good friends. You each looked around for another player. Nobody got hurt, or scarred.

Bill Randall had promised himself that, that other time. He wasn't going to get serious about *any* girl again. Or fall in love. At least, not until he was ready for all the things love meant. Like marriage and a home. Children to bear his name. In five years, perhaps?

He was not ready now.

That night he had begun to feel something deeper. It had frightened him a little. And it had been the same with Valerie Cassidy. It had come from sharing the emotion that her friend's death had caused. The anger, the sadness. . . .

He was out in the street again, and he did not stop. He'd have some coffee and go back to the hospital. End the game now, while it was still a game. Before it stopped being pretense and became reality. Seek a new player before you were hurt. That was best for both of them.

Glen Carew had had a heavy schedule of surgery and made Vaizey's with only a few minutes to spare before closing time. In the elevator going up to the third floor, he thought of Alden Vaizey, whom he had left checking surgical patients in the Recovery Room back at County.

Vaizey was not in the same class as Roy Flagg as an anesthesiologist. He had realized that in the first ten minutes of the first case on the afternoon schedule. He did not have Flagg's judgment or instinctive response to a situation. Vaizey had to be *told*.

He believed that Vaizey always would have to be told. He remembered a famous surgeon during his own internship, who had said that good anesthesiologists were born, not made.

There was truth in that. It was the same argument as Flagg's "interest" put another way. Yet Vaizey hadn't been that bad. Carter might be better one day, but Carter was no better than Alden Vaizey right now. In a comparison, Vaizey was ahead. He had the mechanics, but he just did not have what Flagg had described as "interest."

Carew weaved through the crowd on the third floor toward the same counter where Randall had shopped only a short time back. Waiting to be served, he glanced across at the general office and found himself looking at a pretty blonde girl sitting behind a typewriter. Her hair had caught his attention. Beneath the fluorescent lights it had a golden sheen. Still waiting, he looked again. The girl was staring at him now, he found, and as he looked she raised a hand in greeting and smiled. He recognized her then. Bill Randall's date at the wedding reception. Valerie—? Valerie Cassidy.

"Yes, sir?"

Carew became aware that a clerk was waiting for his order. The man's eyes had a knowing look as they followed the direction of his stare.

"It doesn't matter. I'll come back later." He hesitated. "Isn't the blonde girl typing over there Miss Cassidy?"

"Yes, sir."

"Thank you." Carew was already walking toward the office counter. He watched the girl's eyes widen, and she stood up quickly and came to meet him. She had green eyes, he saw, and she looked as though she had been crying.

He said, "It *is* Miss Cassidy, isn't it? You've probably forgotten, but we met at Dr. Flagg's wedding." He smiled. "You were with Bill Randall!"

"I haven't forgotten you, Dr. Carew. I don't forget easily."

"I was hoping you might spare me a little of your time. There was something I wanted to ask you."

"Oh?" Her expression was a little doubtful.

He said quickly, "About Carol Vincent. Bill told me how you felt. I thought you'd be willing to help me, if you could."

"How, Doctor?"

He lowered his voice. "Miss Cassidy, what happened to your friend was a form of homicide. In a way it's involved us all at the hospital. Not legally, but morally. I want to talk to you about her."

She wet her lips with the pink tip of her tongue and the green eyes tried to hide a sudden fear. "The police have already done that. I told them everything I knew."

"They questioned hospital staff also. The whole place

73

has been in a turmoil. But so far they haven't turned up anything useful."

"What makes you think you can do better?"

Carew frowned. "It occurred to me that, as a doctor, I might learn something they did not have the medical experience to appreciate."

"Oh?" She looked away. "Well, at least I'm flattered that someone I met at the wedding remembers me!"

"Which means?"

She looked at him. "Dr. Randall was in here a few minutes ago. He seemed to have forgotten."

Carew looked his surprise. "Really? I thought you two—?"

He broke off embarrassed.

The girl smiled. So it hadn't been a pass. She couldn't doubt his sincerity. She shook her head, answering his question literally. "It started as a casual date. I don't know why Bill Randall asked me. He must be—impulsive. But he *was* awfully good to me that night. I was upset. He made it bearable. But I haven't seen him since, or heard from him until a few minutes ago when he bought some things at the counter where I saw you. He just waved, and walked away. But that's understandable. I must have spoiled his night."

He said defensively, "Bill isn't like that."

"Then perhaps there's an explanation for him not calling. For the way he just waved and walked away." There was bitterness in her voice. "Not that it matters!" She shrugged. "As I told you, Doctor, it was just a casual date." She glanced up at the clock, the movement stopping his embarrassed protest. "I'll have to go now, Doctor. I have letters to finish. Suppose you wait for me outside the store? I'll be through here in another four or five minutes."

He nodded. "Perhaps we could talk over a cup of coffee? There's a coffee bar in the next block."

"Why not my apartment? Carol's things are there. And you might want to check her stuff. The police did."

She smiled, and turned quickly away. She was already typing furiously as he walked toward the elevators.

He glanced back before he stepped inside. She was watching him, smiling as she changed a sheet of paper. She

74

waved it at him in a gesture that was as warm and friendly as her smile.

Glen Carew was puzzled. He had thought Valerie Cassidy just the type for Bill Randall. He still thought so. And the signs of tears beneath her eyes—?

The thought occurred to him that it might have been a lovers' quarrel, and she was a girl on the rebound. But she had been too calm, too self-assured.

It had meant little to either of them. It was a pity though. A girl like Valerie Cassidy could be good for Bill Randall. Or any man.

CHAPTER SEVEN

"IT'S NOT very big," Valerie Cassidy said, as Carew followed her inside. "But it's clean and convenient, and it fits in with a working girl's budget." She smiled up at him, warm and friendly as she closed the door.

"I like it," he said, looking around. "You've added little things of your own and given it personality."

"Well, it's encouraging to find someone likes it. Mind if I take off my shoes? By the end of the day my feet kill me."

"I know how you feel. Sure! Go ahead."

Opening a door that led out of the living room, she said over her shoulder, "I shared this bathroom with Carol. One to each two apartments. Connecting doors."

The sound of running water came from behind the half-open door. Carew sat on the low divan and lit a cigarette.

"Don't mind the place. It's usually tidier than this, but Carol's stuff makes a difference. No room for it anywhere else. I suppose the police will take it eventually. But in the meantime, I told the janitor he could put her bags in here."

"Won't her relatives claim them?"

"No. Carol was an orphan. Reared in a convent in Canada. Did you know she was Canadian?"

"Someone said Illinois."

"After Canada. Chicago. Then here. Didn't the police tell you that at the hospital? They checked."

"They don't give away much information," he said. He was studying a pile of bags in the corner behind the door. All were new.

Valerie came back into the room. She had taken off her stockings and slipped her bare feet into a pair of soft, snowy white slippers. She followed the direction of his stare.

"Carol must've bought them just before she left Chicago."

"Expensive looking," he murmured. "What did she do in Chicago?"

"Owned a little dress shop. She ran it herself. Not exactly high fashion. Catered to bachelor girls like— well, like herself, and like me. She lived in an apartment like this. Worked alone and lived alone. Maybe that's why the police haven't been able to turn up anything in Chicago."

"You seem well informed."

She nodded. "Ed Fisher told me. He's a friend of Bill Randall's and I suppose he felt he could tell me things."

"How long was your friend here?"

"Two weeks."

"That doesn't seem long for two people to become close friends."

She looked at him quickly. "No? How long does it take?"

"Not very long sometimes. If you are both lonely."

Her eyes were sad, remembering. "The night she moved in, I heard her being sick in the bathroom. I can't say that attracted me. But afterward I heard her crying. When you hear someone crying like that, sort of sobbing with a hurt sound . . . alone . . . you feel they need a friend."

"You went in?"

"Yes. She'd almost fainted. I helped her. After that, I think she used to look forward to me coming home evenings. I don't believe she'd ever had a friend before. Not a real friend. If it hadn't happened the way it did, I'm

77

sure she'd have told me a lot more about herself. If only she'd *waited!* Or *talked* to me about it!"

"She didn't?"

"Not a word about anything like that. But she must've loved him. It wasn't just . . ." Her green eyes were hostile suddenly. "Men are—!"

"Some men," he said quietly.

"Carol was shy. She would have been a virgin. She must have been."

He nodded. "She was. Not very long before. Six weeks perhaps."

Her eyes widened. "You can tell that?"

"There was an autopsy." He changed the subject. "She was only here two weeks?"

"I'll tell you what I told the police. If you don't believe *me*—check with the superintendent. He collects the rent, and runs this place."

Carew grinned. "Did I look as though I disbelieved you?"

"You repeated it."

"It's important, Valerie."

"The police must've asked me the same thing a dozen times. Ed Fisher said they wanted to be sure because they'd check arrivals in town that day. Ed said there had to be a reason for her coming here. It might be whoever —killed her. There must've been a link, a contact. Someone she knew in Chicago, who knew someone here. Maybe the man who got her into trouble. Maybe a friend who knew a friend. . . . That sort of thing. If it was that, the going would be real tough, Ed said. But if *he* sent her, there might be something she'd keep. A letter. A written address. Or he could have come down *with* her. Am I making myself clear?"

"Clear enough. Go on."

"Ed said when something like that happens to a girl like Carol, they just go away as though it's a holiday. And come back when it's over. He thought Carol would have just closed her shop, or left someone else in charge."

"That sounds reasonable."

Valerie shook her head. "They checked, and found

78

she'd *sold* the shop. She had ten thousand dollars transferred to a Calco bank before she left Chicago."

"That seems a lot of money for a small dress shop."

"Some of it she'd saved. She got six thousand for the shop, stock, and good will. She had a good steady clientele. The rest of the money she'd saved over the period she was in Chicago."

"You think it was *her* money?"

"I know it was. She wouldn't take money from any man."

"Did she draw out any large sums of money while she was here?"

"The police checked that. No, she didn't. Just what it cost her to live. She'd draw money as she wanted it. And she had a charge account at Vaizey's."

"She saw nobody here that you know about?" Carew asked.

"The superintendent, me, people in the shops. . . ."

"What did she do all day?"

"I don't know," Valerie said, frowning. "The police questioned the super. He said she seldom went out, and that nobody came to visit her that he saw or heard. And believe me, that man has good eyes and good ears. She read a lot. That big case is full of her books." She gestured toward the bags. "Want to take a look? I have the keys."

Carew shook his head. "No. I don't think I'll bother, Valerie."

"My friends call me Val. Any more questions, or shall I brew us some coffee?"

He stubbed his cigarette on a small ash tray. "Did Fisher mention any leads? Or say what the police intended to do next?"

"Only that they'd find him. But it might take time. They're sure the man is in Chicago."

Carew frowned. "I wonder if it has occurred to the police as strange that a man with as little . . . principle, would desert a young woman with ten thousand dollars in the bank? He could as easily have married her."

She shrugged. "They figure he was married. Some wealthy guy who gave her the contact and left her to it. Anything else, Sherlock Holmes?"

Carew laughed suddenly. "Yes. I could use that cup of coffee, Val."

He had eased the tension and she smiled. "I know how you feel about this, Doctor. Bill Randall was the same. I guess a good doctor gets so wrapped up in saving life, in bringing new life into the world and all that, that he has an instinctive hatred for people who destroy life. That's why you wanted to question me, isn't it?"

"I hadn't thought of it like that," Carew admitted. "It's just something you feel. But you're right, Val."

"Well, you don't have to be angry with me. And I'm tired of calling you Doctor. I'm going to call you Glen. Any objections—Glen?"

"I'd like that," he said sincerely.

She placed two coffee cups on a tray and frowned at the percolator. "A watched percolator never climbs the tube! Like cream and cinnamon, Viennese style?"

"It could spoil me for hospital coffee."

"I'll spoil you then." She liked him better smiling. Momentarily, he looked boyish. But his anger was still there. It was a deep, controlled anger, not like the more youthful fury that Bill Randall had shown. She shivered suddenly.

"If I was the man who killed Carol," she thought, "I'd keep well away from Glen Carew!"

And the way he was looking now . . .

She said aloud, "Did you learn anything from what I told you, Glen? Because if you did and I can add to it— just ask."

"Perhaps, Val. I don't know. I'm only a doctor. If anything else occurs to me, I'll ask."

She brought coffee and cookies and sat down on the divan beside him. She drew the low coffee table in closer.

"Now you're evading what I asked, aren't you? If you don't feel you can trust me, that's okay. But if *you* feel badly about what happened to Carol, how do you think I feel? I'm only pushing it because I want to help."

Carew's dark brows drew together. "At the hospital, everyone believes the same as the police. That it was done for money. That the man is a professional abortionist and will do the same again. They're hoping for that. The next time they'll be looking for it. They'll catch him."

"When *another* girl dies?" Her green eyes widened.

"No. When another girl lives."

She was staring at him. "I see! Only most girls wouldn't admit it, or talk about it. Not even under pressure by the police. Questioned, they'd lie. And if the police don't have a witness—what *can* they do? They don't have a case."

She was shrewd, all right. Carew nodded.

"You don't believe he'll attempt another. Why not?" she asked, frowning. "People like that will do anything, if the price is okay."

"It doesn't seem to have occurred to the police that the man who procured the drug and injected it, and the man she—loved, might be one man. Not two."

"But he's in Chicago. Isn't he?" she asked in amazement. "And wouldn't he have to be someone with experience, to get the hypodermic and the drug and know how to use them? Or are you saying that her lover is a *doctor?*"

"I don't know what he is," Carew said slowly. "I didn't think of it in that way. But I suppose he could be some sort of doctor. Morally weak. Professionally—certainly not well trained in obstetrics or gynecology. Perhaps only a student—or possibly someone who could have specialized in another branch of medicine and not had anything to do with gynecology or obstetrics since interning. A man like that could mistake the diagnosis. But I'm sure of one thing. Either he was here before your friend or she knew that he was coming here. That has to be the reason why she sold her little shop and transferred her money here. She did that to be with him."

She was frowning, her coffee forgotten. "You could be right! That might explain why she never had visitors or went out much until the night she disappeared."

"Yes, it could. Don't you think that if he had come here earlier, if he had been here when Carol arrived, you would have known?"

"Yes," she whispered, her eyes narrowing as she stared across the room. "Yes! A woman can hide some things, but not the way she feels when she's meeting a lover. She would have been happier. Excited. Glowing. But Carol was moody, quiet, awfully sad. She said nothing. Sometimes I'd hear her crying. Glen, that was because he wasn't here. He hadn't arrived. Maybe she'd started to doubt that he would come."

"A woman *waiting?*"

"Yes! I see it now. Say, you're smart!" She looked at him admiringly. "And you learned that from the way I answered your questions. Ed Fisher and the other police asked the same questions, but formed different conclusions from what I told them. And when Carol died, the creep must've run for home and Chicago. Will you tell the police? Say, maybe they can check on who left Calco for Chicago about then? Plane, railroad bookings, gas station attendants who might remember someone who drove East. Someone with an Illinois license plate."

"Or maybe he's still here," Carew said grimly. "Maybe he *lives* here, and that's why she followed him."

He watched her young face harden. "If he is, I want to help you find him."

Carew fixed her with a long, searching look. "At Vaizey's you might be in a position to do that. A lot of people pass through the store, have accounts there. Isn't it just possible that someone might have opened an account around the time she disappeared?—someone from Chicago, giving Chicago credit references?"

She returned his steady gaze. "I'll check it, Glen. It's a good thought."

"Good girl!"

She smiled, pleased. "We should go into the detective business. Only, don't forget, Glen—it all falls down if there were two of them. If one man in Chicago who was the father sent her to another man in Calco who had the drug and the knowledge—"

Glen Carew shook his head. "It doesn't fall down, Val. When your friend died, she was five weeks pregnant. Everyone seems to have forgotten that time factor. She was here for two weeks. Therefore, when she came here from Chicago she *didn't know*. And neither did *he*. She came here to be near him. For *that* reason she sold the shop and came to live here. Not for any other. That came later."

She was staring at him. "Then if he didn't *know,* he

82

would have had to get the drug here? Unless he already had it—"

"And the hypodermic—unless he already had that."

"That narrows the field, doesn't it?" She was staring at him, wide-eyed.

Carew nodded soberly. "It does! Very much." He put down his empty cup and stood up. "I'll look after the medical angle, you see what you can find out at Vaizey's. Right?"

She nodded. "Will you tell the police what you believe?"

She was walking beside him to the door of the apartment. She was taller than he had thought. An attractive girl. A girl of warmth and quick friendships. A sincere girl. Carew felt that he had known her a long time as he watched her smile up at him.

"I'd rather wait until I have something to tell them that isn't just . . . abstract."

She said thoughtfully, "Yes. Let's be sure first." She put her hand on the door. "When will I see you again?"

"Mostly when I'm free I drive downtown. Vaizey's is a regular call."

"I'll be looking for you," she whispered. Watching him go, hope and confidence stirred within her. Dr. Glen Carew would never fail anyone.

CHAPTER EIGHT

THE Calco County Hospital Flying Ambulance held a steady line of flight above forested ranges, with the glint of water ahead. Their patient lay on his left side, a nasal gastric aspiration tube held in place by adhesive plaster. Dr. Glen Carew watched him anxiously. The man was very thin, lines of worry showing plainly on the leathery face that had faded to a yellowish tinge through what had been a heavy suntan.

"I'll have you on the asphalt in well under an hour, Glen." Max Addison's voice was deliberately low.

"Good!"

"Old Tomlinson is as tough as a range mustang," Addison said in a louder voice. "Take more than an ulcer to stop you, eh, Ted?"

The man on the stretcher nodded his head weakly.

Addison raised his eyebrows in silent question at Carew. Carew shook his head slightly. A lot would depend on the spread of the fluid leaking from a perforated peptic ulcer. There is no abdominal catastrophe where successful operation is more dependent upon early diagnosis than a perforated ulcer. And Tomlinson had probably nursed his in secret for a long time, growing accustomed to the nagging pain, becoming more morose, but never giving in or seeking medical attention.

Not until the pain had become so acute, the vomiting

of blood so frightening, that he had thought himself dying and had sent the emergency call to Calco.

His family had put the time of acute pain at eight hours earlier, and for the first ten hours after perforation, the peritoneal cultures were usually sterile. But if it *had* perforated earlier than that, the cavity could already be infected by invading bacteria.

It was anybody's guess right now whether Tomlinson's ulcer had already spread its infection beyond the possibility of corrective therapy, even after successful surgery.

The perforation ruled out the use of morphine or its derivatives to relieve pain, forcing Carew to use only sedatives until the hospital was reached and the diagnosis confirmed. But he was fighting the possible spread of infection at once by the gastric aspiration, trying to keep the leakage through the perforation to a minimum, and localized.

He glanced back again, and met the eyes of the nurse sitting beside Tomlinson. He smiled tentatively, but she looked away.

"How is he now, Miss Forrest?"

Her smile was for the patient. "Just fine, aren't you, Mr. Tomlinson?"

"I'll beat it!" the man gritted, his voice muffled and made sick by the rubber tube draining fluid from his stomach at regular intervals.

Carew glanced at his watch. "We'll aspirate again in a few minutes, Miss Forrest. I'll come back to help."

"Drunk too much bad whisky in your day, eh, Ted?" Addison asked jocularly.

"I've got . . . my worries. . . ."

Carew was glad that Tomlinson's toughness enabled him to get the words out. He was going to need all that toughness.

"Must be near the Rubies now, Max, eh?" Tomlinson said, anxious now to end this painful journey.

"Right ahead," Addison told him cheerfully. "I can see Cherry Lake, a couple of guys fishing."

"Lucky stiffs," Tomlinson muttered. "Got me some land down there once. Always reckoned on buildin' a cabin, but ain't ever got around . . . to it."

"You will!" Addison assured him. "One of those guys down there is aiming a camera up at us. You'll be like that, Ted. Taking shots of all the big cutthroat trout you haul out of Cherry Lake. And telling tall stories about it afterward. Right, Glen?"

Carew said, "Sure he will!" He was unclipping his seat belt. "Hold her steady, Max, we're going to aspirate again. Ready, Kathie?"

She nodded. "Ready, Doctor."

It was hard to hold anger against him when he looked at her like that. She returned his smile involuntarily as he stood up.

At County Hospital the surgeons in the Emergency Room prepared for the coming operation.

Dan Ward took a blood sample for Pathology and the matching for possible blood transfusion. Carl Lindemann, frowning and intent, began the cutdown of a vein for the saline-dextrose infusion almost as soon as the patient, Ted Tomlinson, was wheeled back from the X-ray room.

Miss Flint aspirated the stomach at intervals through the tube already in place. They were a smoothly working team under the guidance of the surgeon, Dr. Glen Carew, as he told them what he wanted.

In minutes, Dr. Pete Kane, the radiologist, was ready with still dripping X rays to show Carew, and the patient was being trundled toward the operating room annex to be shaved and prepared for the operation.

"How is it, Pete?" Carew asked Kane as he walked into the X-ray room.

"Typical crescent-shaped gas shadow, Dr Carew," Kane said, grinning. His pencil tip traced a translucent area beneath the cage of ribs on the right side. "Confirm your diagnosis?"

Carew nodded, studying the dripping plates. "Peptic ulcer on the right side, and perforated. Have these set up in the O.R., please, Pete."

"They're as good as in the view boxes," Kane said cheerfully. "Well, the guy's lucky—!"

"With a perforated ulcer?"

"I'll say he is!" Kane said, grinning. "Here's a guy two hundred air miles from a hospital, and his ulcer per-

86

forates. He is three hundred miles away by the kind of roads they have down there. But he's here and alive, and he's got a chance, hasn't he?"

Carew nodded soberly. Sometimes he forgot the importance of Max Addison's Flying Ambulance. But without it, and without the immediate gastric aspiration he had been able to give, the man now being prepared for surgery would still be far down the trail, bumping over barely formed desert roads with every yard agony, every mile lessening his chance for life. Bacterial infection would have started and become widespread, to cause a diffuse peritonitis that no medical skill could correct.

He walked quickly back into the Emergency Room.

"I have the blood group, Doctor," Dan Ward said eagerly. "It's O. A flask of O Rh-negative is being sent through to the O.R."

"What about the culture?"

"There's the beginning of a streptococcal infection. Dr. Maitland thinks it's about twelve hours since it perforated. Bacteriostatic effect of the stomach acid no longer present to help him."

"Tomlinson *was* lucky!" Carew said quietly. "Well, we've kept it localized. And we started penicillin in the plane. He has a good chance now. Fill me in on the surgical team."

"Dr. Lindemann is assisting you, Doctor. I'm scrubbing to stand by—" He hesitated. "If that's okay with you?"

Carew nodded. He knew the reason for that hesitation, and deliberately ignored it. "Fine, Dan. I was going to ask you to. What about anesthesia?"

"Dr. Vaizey!" The young intern's face was wooden. "He's probably prepping the patient now in the annex."

Carew glanced at his watch. "Good. I want to start as soon as possible. Will you tell Miss Spain that, please? Then scrub. I've already talked to Dr. Vaizey about the anesthesia."

"Miss Spain is ready. Dr. Lindemann had her prepare the O.R. as soon as we got the call through Calco Tower." Dan Ward's expression had changed to undisguised admiration. "Dr. Lindemann said that if you had diagnosed a perforated peptic ulcer, it'd be a sure thing. He's scrubbing now. He said he'll take over the preparation of the operative area while you're scrubbing. Time is the essence of the contract with a perforation, isn't it?"

"It's the essence of life," Carew said, grinning. "So we'll leave the other definition to the legal eagles. Go through and help Dr. Lindemann when you've scrubbed."

"Yes, sir."

Carew walked into the annex of the Emergency O.R., his smile fading.

Alden Vaizey looked up quickly. His gray eyes had a hard look that softened a little now as he recognized Glen Carew.

"I'm about ready to take him through, Doctor."

"Fine." Carew bent over the patient. "How do you feel, Mr. Tomlinson?"

"Pretty . . . good."

"He just signed the permission slip for the operation, Doctor," Vaizey said carelessly. "He's had Demerol, as you instructed. He's in no pain now."

Carew nodded to the nurse. "You can take him in now. We start with a local anesthetic, as you may know."

"A local?" the sick man said, roused to alarm despite the Demerol. "I don't want a local—nobody ever said anything about a local for this!"

Carew glanced at Vaizey, controlling anger. "I thought Dr. Vaizey would have explained this to you," he said.

"Well, he damned well didn't! And now you got me helpless here and you're talking about giving me only a local!"

Alden Vaizey flushed. He came forward quickly. "I'm sorry, Mr. Tomlinson. There's nothing for you to worry about, I assure you. You'll neither see nor feel anything at all. You'll be having combined anesthesia—first a local anesthetic that will completely deaden all sensation, and then a general anesthetic into a vein of your arm that will put you completely to sleep. You'll be nice and drowsy even before you have the general anesthetic. You can take my word for it—not one moment of the entire procedure is going to bother you."

The sick man looked at Carew. "Is that right, Doc?"

Carew nodded, noting that the Demerol was now working more effectively—Tomlinson was slurring his words and visibly relaxing under its influence "Absolutely right," he assured him. "You haven't a thing to worry about." But Carew was concerned—not for his patient, but for Vaizey's omissions. The rancher's question had clearly expressed confidence in the surgeon and not in the anesthesiologist. And it was important that a patient have confidence in the anesthesiologist. Roy Flagg would not have made a mistake like that. Or even Carter. . . .

Carew watched somberly as two nurses trundled the patient on the stretcher through the double doors into the operating room. In there, nurses under instruction were working quietly, so that the clatter of instruments would not make the patient apprehensive.

He looked back at Vaizey. "Dr. Lindemann will prepare the operative area. I want a nurse to watch the dextrose-saline fluid therapy infusion. The flask must not be allowed to empty."

Alden Vaizey nodded, red-faced. "I'm aware of that, Doctor. I'll start the infusion at once."

"There's no haste for it. I'll be ten minutes scrubbing. His general condition will improve as soon as it starts though, so no delay either. We'll continue it throughout the operation, and afterward in the Recovery Room. Right?"

Vaizey smiled. "Yes, Dr. Carew. I'll watch that." His assurance had returned. He added, "I did have experience in anesthesia in Chicago. Although there, we usually gave them a flask of plasma before the dextrose-saline."

"His blood pressure happens to be adequate," Carew remarked stiffly. "One hundred and ten systolic. Otherwise we'd do the same here. Is there anything more you want to know about the anesthesia?"

"I don't think so." Vaizey frowned, considering. "I'm using two syringes for the pentothal. I'll have the two injections of a five percent solution ready before we start."

"Make sure you don't inject it into the tube too high up."

Vaizey said patiently, "I inject into the lumen of the rubber tube like a vein. I'll need a nurse to watch the patient while I inject the pentothal."

"Miss Spain will look after that."

"At Chicago, we used a spinal. This is a British technique, isn't it?"

"And a good one," Carew said. "But there's a tendency to cyanosis. You'll have to be prepared for that. Inject the first ampule very slowly. Wait five minutes before you start the second. Have oxygen ready. Right?"

"Yes, I understand. We infiltrate the abdominal wall with procaine first?"

"Yes, procaine, as I told you," Carew said drily. "The patient is still conscious. We open the skin of the abdomen to infiltrate the rectus sheaths. It's best this way, in my opinion. But many people are uneasy about locals."

Vaizey colored. His glance at Carew was apologetic. "I'm sorry, Glen—Dr. Carew!" He looked young, and almost gauche suddenly. "You're right, of course. Sometimes I act like a student."

"Or as though you're not really interested," Carew said.

"But I am!" Alden Vaizey answered quickly. "Maybe I wasn't at first. In student days, as an intern. . . . But when you become a resident all that seems to change. All the things you've learned and practiced fall into place. And that's medicine. *That's what I want.* Nothing else!"

"Are you sure of that?" Carew asked bluntly.

Vaizey shook his head in a hopeless gesture. "Why else would I be *here?* I don't have to work in a crummy county hospital for the pittance Prentice calls salary! I own a major interest in Vaizey stores. I own—but the rest doesn't matter. I'm a wealthy man. I don't have to work, to take the insults I've taken here. But I want to practice medicine. Can't you understand that? My God, Carew, I thought you were a dedicated doctor, a surgeon who'd sooner practice his profession than do anything else in life. I thought *you* would understand. . . ."

"I'm trying to," Carew said crisply.

"I chose anesthesiology because it's the particular branch of medicine that I believe I'm best suited to. I don't have your skill as a surgeon, nor could I ever acquire it. I don't have Maitland's type of inquiring mind to tackle pathology. Or Lindsay's sympathy and understanding of women to take on obstetrics. But anesthesiology—that's something different. And I came here to prac-

90

tice it because this is my town. I was born here, and my father before me. I grew up with the people here, and I want to help them. Can't you understand that?"

Carew's serious brown eyes looked away. "Yes, Dr. Vaizey, I believe I understand that—now." He glanced at his watch. "The patient must be almost ready. I'll have to scrub."

The patient breathed quickly, respiration and the shallow heartbeat quickened by a fear that the Demerol could not quite dull. Lindemann was talking soothingly to him as he swabbed the operative area with scarlet antiseptic solution. Ward was already starting the intravenous drip of fluid therapy from the flask in the infusion stand.

Carew checked the drip rate automatically, but already briefed, Ward was setting it at fifty to the minute in preparation for the pentothal.

Supervising the aspirating of fluid from the stomach, Carew was watching a different Alden Vaizey suddenly.

"You're going to feel the prick of a needle as I inject the local anesthetic to deaden pain, Mr. Tomlinson," the anesthesiologist was saying cheerfully. "But that's all it will be—the prick of a needle. And you'll feel a little numb around the area afterward."

"I reckon I can stand that," the patient muttered sickly, "now I'm a little more used to the idea, Dr.—is it Vaizey?"

"That's right."

"Heard somebody calling you that. You old John Vaizey's boy?"

"Right again, Mr. Tomlinson."

"Sort of makes you one of us, eh?" Tomlinson was losing his stiffness, his tension. He was starting to relax.

"I'd like it to be that way," Alden Vaizey said. His gray eyes met Carew's deliberately as the small pump sucked dry, and Carew gestured to the nurse to stop pumping.

Carew nodded approval briefly before his eyes checked the infiltration. Vaizey was gesturing to the taut abdomen before he stepped back and Carew moved into his place. He had injected procaine now from the navel to the sternum, anesthetizing the area of skin.

Carew held out his hand silently to Kathie Forrest as

she slid her instrument table over the patient's legs. The first scalpel came into his hand.

The taut skin parted with very little bleeding as Carew made the first incision. The anesthesiologist came back with a new syringe and needle as Carew undercut the skin layer. Lindemann swabbed it clear of the seeping blood and held the edges back with forceps, exposing the sheaths of rectus muscle beneath.

Still talking to his patient, Alden Vaizey injected deeper, the procaine now deadening the muscles covering the peritoneal cavity. He was working quickly and efficiently, aware of Carew's watching eyes, and of the occasional hostile glance of Lindemann and Dan Ward.

"Sure I remember you now, Mr. Tomlinson," Vaizey was saying. "You used to bring in cattle to the railroad. I was just a kid then, always getting into trouble for watching the cattle down at the loading pens. I even remember your brand. It was a *T* in some sort of box, wasn't it?"

"Diamond T," Tomlinson said, delighted. "We sold that outfit years ago. Fancy you remembering!"

"I want you to relax now," Vaizey said. "Miss Spain is going to talk to you while I put you to sleep. She's going to ask you to count slowly. Pretend you're counting cattle through a chute. You'll get to twenty, or maybe thirty, then you'll fall asleep. And when you wake up you'll be in bed in your room. No more ulcer. No more pain. Right?"

"Sure, Doc!"

Carew's eyes checked automatically as Vaizey swabbed the rubber tube of the infusion set with antiseptic, sterilizing it so that the needle he was about to insert into the tube could not acquire infection from unsterile rubber. At the head of the table Miss Spain, the O.R. charge nurse, was talking quietly to the patient now and he was starting to count in a shaky voice.

The needle pierced the rubber tube. Alden Vaizey looked at Glen Carew. The surgeon nodded approval.

"Slowly," he said. "Very slowly. . . ."

Today, Alden Vaizey was working as smoothly as Roy Flagg could have done. Carew turned back in satisfaction to his own work.

He had been cutting steadily as Vaizey talked, with

92

Lindemann silently matching his needs. The incision grew longer and deeper long before that weakening voice from the head of the operating table faded to silence.

He had completed the midline incision and was ready to open the peritoneum. Towels bordered it, the green stained here and there as a bleeder spurted before Lindemann could catch it with hemostats.

With the procaine in full operation upon the wall of the abdomen, the man fading into unconsciousness felt nothing. Carew heard the distinct pop of escaping gas as he tented the peritoneum and incised its membrance.

He must work a little faster to expose the perforation, as with each respiration now, infectious fluid would gush through the perforation uncontrolled. The rubber tube of another small aspirator came into his hand. With Lindemann's help he began clearing the cavity of fluid already loose in there.

He looked up. "How is he, Dr. Vaizey?"

"Pressure unchanged, Doctor. Respiration is shallower, but his pulse is still good."

"Give the readings, Doctor."

Vaizey gave them quickly. Embarrassed, he added, "He's slightly cyanosed. I'm administering oxygen."

"When his color improves, inject more pentothal. I'd like him a little deeper."

"Yes, Doctor."

"Abdominal pack, Miss Forrest."

The moist pack came into Carew's right hand, and he watched Lindemann clear the last of the obscuring fluid by sponging. Lindemann moved back, and he bent to grasp the stomach near its greater curvature, his gloved fingers drawing it out gently by the moist pad.

Another moist sponge came into his left hand and he sought the perforation as he drew out the reddish-veined organ, sponging it clear of infecting fluid as it drew through the incision.

"There it is!" Lindemann's voice said in relief.

"Hold it in traction, Dr. Lindemann."

Lindemann's hands took over, holding, sponging the area clear as Carew examined the small, white-edged hole beneath the greater curvature. He nodded satisfaction.

"We can clean it up, close it with three sutures, and

reinforce it with a flap of the omentum!" he said, pleased.

"The cyanosis is clearing, Dr. Carew," Vaizey's voice said eagerly. "His color is improving."

Carew spared a quick glance. "That's fine, Dr. Vaizey. Good work! Dr. Ward, we're going to need an extra hand in here. Move in. Miss Spain, will you watch the infusion?"

The first suture of catgut touched his palm, the round, curved needle already threaded and ready for use. He placed the first suture. The small, circular hole closed with the second suture, was made secure with the third.

He found a flap of the omentum and laid it over the tested suture line. He fastened it in place as an extra seal with interrupted, unabsorbable stitches.

Around the table he heard the soft breaths of relieved tension, as he looked for other ulcers and found none.

"All right," he said calmly. "We'll close with drainage. Another injection of pentothal, Dr. Vaizey, and that should be the last."

Tomlinson would live. For the surgical team, there was satisfaction in that. Suction had cleared the peritoneal cavity of infected fluid from the punctured stomach. Antibiotics would clear any small pocket of infection left. The ulcer was gone now, the perforation closed by surgery.

They talked about it cheerfully as they washed and then changed from their scrub suits in the doctors' locker room. Lindemann and Ward were together in a corner. They were taking their time about changing, because both were going off duty now, with Jimmy Woldman and another intern taking over Emergency.

Vaizey had taken the stretcher through into the Recovery Room. Dressing quickly, Carew thought about Alden Vaizey. He could not fault his work today. Perhaps Roy Flagg had been right. If Vaizey *was* interested, he could be brilliant.

"All right, so he was good today," Ward's angry young voice broke into Carew's thoughts. "I'll admit that. Dr. Lindemann. He *was* good. But what I'd like to know is —why couldn't he have been as good the night that girl died?"

Ward stopped abruptly, and Carew saw the reason for that as he looked up quickly. Alden Vaizey was standing just inside the door staring at Ward, his face white with fury.

"Were you referring to me, Ward?" he asked in a low voice.

"I was," Ward said defiantly. He straightened from buckling his belt and glared at Vaizey. "And I wasn't saying it because you weren't in the room, Doctor. I'll repeat it now. If you were so damned good in there today, why the hell didn't you do something about the Vincent girl that other night—instead of just standing around?"

"You sonofabitch!" Vaizey snarled. "Here's your answer!"

He took a long step and swung a punch that knocked Ward down.

Carew said sharply, "Stop that!" He caught Ward's arms as the intern bounced up and rushed at Vaizey, a trickle of blood from his cut lip starting to smear the side of his chin.

"Let him go, Doctor!" Vaizey shouted. "I'll fix that damn young smart aleck once and for all!" He was moving toward Carew and the young intern. Lindemann grabbed Vaizey and held him back.

"Cool down," Carew said grimly. "Both of you!"

"He called me a sonofabitch," Ward panted. "He hit me—"

Carew's voice cracked across the room. "Any more punches, and neither of you will be working at this hospital. Is that clear?"

He felt the tension go out of the young intern. He released him slowly.

"Anyone who calls me that has to expect to get something back," Ward muttered. "And now's as good a time as any."

"There'll be no fighting!" Carew upheld his authority.

"This is something personal," Vaizey said, still scowling. "I've heard enough from him."

"I sent you to the Recovery Room, Doctor," Carew said.

"So you could slander me here?" he suggested sarcastically.

"Go back to the Recovery Room. You have a patient there."

"Carter's taken over—"

"I sent *you* there—not Carter."

"You're making it an order, Doctor?"

"I am," Carew said, controlling anger. "By God, and if you don't obey it, you're through here."

Alden Vaizey's lips tightened. "There'll be another day," he said to Ward. He walked out and closed the door hard.

"Dr. Carew, he insulted you, too," Ward said. "You should've let me hit him!"

"Are you setting yourself up as an authority on tubal pregnancy, Dr. Ward?" Carew said coldly.

"Eh?" Ward said, startled. "Of course I'm not. But I was there, and—"

"How many cases of ruptured tubal pregnancy have you seen as an intern, *Doctor?*"

Ward stared at him. He was seeing a different Glen Carew now from the surgeon whose skill he had admired in the operating room. "You know damned well I haven't seen any in the few months I've been here—"

"Did you diagnose it, or did you diagnose criminal abortion of a normal pregnancy?"

"I made a mistake," Ward said reluctantly.

Carew nodded. "Exactly. Now, I suggest you put your coat on and go back to the residence. And in the future, be sure you're right and you can prove you're right before you accuse another doctor of what amounts to criminal negligence."

"I might have known . . ." Ward said angrily. He thrust his arms into his coat and stalked out.

Lindemann looked after him, frowning. "You were a little hard on him, I thought, Glen."

"Would you have agreed with what he said about Vaizey?"

Lindemann shook his head. "Not unless I was sure it was right. And we can't be sure. I told you—I wasn't there. No. We all have too much to lose. The years of study, of training, the ideal. . . ."

"Ward's all right," Carew said wearily. "I like that boy. But he has to learn control."

"And Dr. Vaizey?"

96

Carew frowned. "Today, as Ward said, he was very good. He has possibilities as an anesthesiologist, as a doctor . . . but as a man—?" He shook his head. "I don't know, Carl."

CHAPTER NINE

GLEN CAREW, following the trim figure of Valerie Cassidy upstairs to her apartment, was aware of an inner restlessness that was not a part of the deep resentment driving him. The resentment had no real point of focus because he could not visualize the man he sought.

But this other feeling had focus. It centered upon the girl climbing the stairs a step ahead of him, her voice slightly breathless when she spoke, her perfume a part of her nearness as they reached the top landing and she put her hand on his arm and laughed.

"If you come up here much more, Glen, this place is going to seem like home to you."

"Worse things could happen to a lonely surgeon," he said.

She looked at him covertly. "Don't tell me *you're* lonely, Glen?"

He frowned suddenly. No, he wasn't lonely. The thought of personal loneliness was something that would never occur to him. He said, "No. I was thinking of Bill Randall when I said that."

"Oh?" She fumbled with the key, opening the door. She laughed. "Not *that* man! Not with—how many pretty nurses do you have at County?"

"Don't believe all the fiction you read about hospital

life," he said, smiling. "The part about love among the splint cupboards isn't true. We're all far too busy."

"You perhaps," she said. "Too busy until you find the right one. But Bill—? I know that man. Would you have me believe that nurses are a race apart? I know some of them. They're women, Glen. Just like the rest of us. Same anatomy, same instincts, same reactions. And doctors do fall in love with them."

She opened the door and watched him come in diffidently. He was, she decided, a little naïve where girls were concerned. But she liked him the better for that.

He said quickly, "Bill Randall isn't interested in any girl at County."

"He isn't interested in any girl, period," she said. "But maybe if you made that plural—? Well, it isn't important to me. Not now."

He looked at her steadily. "It might be very good for you if it was."

"No, Glen. With me it's a dollar spent, and I'm just a working girl. I don't have another right now, and it would be too much to expect that one back. So shall we get on with it? I found out some interesting facts at work today. That's why I called you. But I have to be rid of these shoes first, so make yourself at home. There's Scotch in the cupboard, water and ice in the kitchenette. I like mine drowned *and* frozen, thanks."

Finding the whisky, ice, and water gave him a sense of belonging here. But mixing the drinks, he pushed that thought away.

"I'm here because a girl died," he told himself grimly. "Because I'm trying to find the man who killed her. And Val Cassidy can help me."

"Penny for them, Doctor," she said behind him.

"They weren't important enough to repeat. Except that I remembered suddenly why I'm here. Enough water?"

"Drown it a little more. Another ice cube. That's it. Thank you, Glen. Not for the thoughts—for the drink."

She carried hers to the divan and sat down. Her toes wriggled gratefully inside her slippers. She said, "Now—where were we? Heard of Robert T. Candish?"

"The banker?"

She nodded. "It may not mean anything, but he sponsored her account at Vaizey's."

"If she banked with him, that would be normal procedure. Candish is sixty-five and married, with a grown-up family, and above reproach."

"Too bad," she said. "I've looked through the accounts, and I've asked some of the people at the store if they have heard of anyone having arrived from Chicago in the last six weeks or so, but have had no success. There was the boss, of course."

Carew frowned. "The boss?"

"Alden Vaizey. He doesn't have much to do with the store, but technically he is the boss. He owns this building, too. It's party of Vaizey Investments. Rents and expenses go through some books I looked at. One thing I noticed was Carol's rent for the apartment. She paid the first week in advance. But no more rent was paid after that. I've been wondering all afternoon if someone arranged to pay it for her, then, when she died, didn't."

"Did you find any record of that?"

"Nothing. And Carol wouldn't have let the rent go. She wasn't the type. And Vaizeys are fonder of their pounds of flesh than most landlords. Like it on the dot, in advance. What do you make of that, Glen?" She asked it hopefully.

"Maybe she was upset, and forgot."

Valerie Cassidy shook her head. "Carol had an orderly mind. She would've paid, unless someone else intended to pay it for her."

"Who?"

She looked at the faintly amber drink in her glass reproachfully. "I don't know. There's only . . . Alden Vaizey," she said slowly. "He was working at a Chicago hospital and came back here three or four days before Carol—died."

"But Alden Vaizey is a doctor," Carew said sharply. "He's trying to specialize in anesthesia. And in some ways, he is good."

She looked up at him, surprised somewhat at the tone of his voice. "Okay. I only mentioned it because you *did* say that if it *was* a doctor, he might be someone who specialized and hadn't had much to do with the diagnosis of women's troubles in a long time."

Carew frowned. "I did say that. But not Alden Vaizey. No!"

She touched his arm gently. "Glen, all the girls in town run after Alden Vaizey. He's the best catch in Calco. And he's dated plenty of girls here whenever he came back to town."

"This time?" Carew asked.

"Not this time."

"We've been keeping him too busy at the hospital." Carew's laugh sounded forced.

"No. It started earlier than that. He made a date with Nita Montez the day he arrived back. Nita models fashion clothes at the store, and all the girls are jealous of her, I guess. She boasted about it—because she's that kind of girl. But he phoned her later the same day and called it off. One of the girls on the switchboard listened in. She heard Alden tell Nita he was going down to a cabin on Cherry Lake for a couple of days fishing. He said he'd been working too hard, and needed the rest. She tried to persuade him to take her along. But he just hung up. Nita was furious."

"That's understandable."

She wasn't sure whether he meant Nita's anger or Vaizey's need of rest. She picked up her empty glass, turning it idly between her fingers. "Glen, shouldn't we examine *every* possibility?"

"Yes, of course!"

She said tentatively, "Well, as a doctor, wouldn't Alden Vaizey have access to the drug at the hospital. And a hypodermic?"

"He'd probably have a number of syringes and needles in his personal medical kit. Yes. But access to oxytocic drugs—no. He didn't start at County until an hour or so before Carol Vincent died."

"Could he have brought it from Chicago with him?"

"It would be unlikely," Carew said, frowning. "Only someone specializing in obstetrics would carry it. And he'd have to be in private practice to do that. Besides, we have to remember that the father could not know she was pregnant at that stage."

101

"He could have obtained it at a pharmacy, as a doctor, couldn't he?"

Her persistence was starting to annoy him. "That would be the first police check. All pharmacies. He'd have to be a complete fool to get it at a pharmacy. And he isn't that."

She put down her empty glass and spread her hands in a gesture of resignation. "Okay. Alden Vaizey is *out!* The banker's out. Glen, I just don't have anyone else." She was close to tears. "I tried so hard. I can't think of any other possibilities I can check at the store. And I've talked to every girl in this building. He didn't see Carol *here,* whoever he is. They just met someplace secretly and talked. Or she called him from an outside phone. Then she went to her appointment—and her death."

"And he goes free," Carew growled.

She put her hand on his arm. "That's one thing we have in common, don't we? We want to destroy him!" Her green eyes blazed suddenly, and her fingers tightened on his arm. "I hate him! And it's worse because I can't picture him. I can't visualize what kind of man he is. If he was just someone who did things like that for money. But he could be *anyone!*"

Carew nodded. Her words were an echo of the way he felt.

"That's right," he said. "He could be anyone. And I'm like you, I want him destroyed. Professionally, if he is a professional. But also as a man. I want his freedom taken away, to see him a number in a prison, with as little hope left as he gave your friend."

"Then you've found nothing at the hospital?"

"Dr. Prentice is having all nursing notes in Emergency, Gynecology, and Obstetrics checked. But it can't be done quickly. It means a stock-taking of the supplies of all the oxytocic drugs, and a checking of one against the other. Even then, it isn't exactly evidence at law. It's possible for an intern in the maternity ward, for instance, to give a contracting drug, and then be too busy to write it down. Or a resident."

She was watching him. "Glen, we've got to do something."

102

He glanced at his watch. "I could call Dr. Prentice. He may have the report by now. But even if it does show missing drugs, it isn't going to point to anyone in particular. A lot of nurses, residents, and interns work in Obstetrics. It's the same in Gynecology, where the drugs could be used for hemorrhage. It's the same in Emergency where she died."

She frowned. "But it would point to someone connected with the hospital. Someone who had been in Chicago until just before Carol died."

"You're thinking of Alden Vaizey again—" He broke off.

Nobody at County had been in Chicago until just before Carol Vincent died. Except Alden Vaizey. . . .

"There must be some way we can be sure, Glen," she said slowly. "One way or the other."

He stood up. "I'll call Dr. Prentice. If there are drugs missing, we'll take it from there."

"Thanks, Glen. I'll get us another drink."

Carew walked abruptly to the phone. Making the drinks, she watched him dialing, talking. The tension she had built up within herself as she thought of the man who had caused Carol's death faded slowly. It was better when someone was here with her. It was bearable. Then, she didn't think of Carol as much as she did when she was alone.

"I've got to get away from this place," she thought. "This town, this apartment, Vaizey's. . . ."

She was putting the drinks down as he came back to her. "Anything?" she asked.

"They've finished checking. Six shots short. Pitressin. The same drug they found in Carol Vincent. But that isn't conclusive. Now more checking starts. Interns and residents on the carpet, checking procedures and patients from memory or their own notes. Nurses checking nursing instructions and racking *their* memories. It's possible that all six ampules will be accounted for in time."

"Or that four will be missing. How soon will you know?"

"It could take days." He frowned. "But suppose we go on the premise that four *are* missing? Suppose we *suspect* Vaizey. What then?"

"We tell the police," she said fiercely.

He shook his head. "We'd need real evidence for that. Something more than just suspicion. . . . Access? How did he get it? How *could* he get it in time?"

"He'd have to go to the hospital. Nobody would bring it to him, would they?" she said in her down-to-earth way.

"How could they? He didn't know anyone—Wait! He knew Roy Flagg!"

"But Dr. Flagg is in California."

"And no farther away than your phone," Carew said, remembering. "Roy was starting his new job down there today. And if he isn't at the hospital, they'll have a call number." He got up quickly. "I'll take care of the charges."

He put in the call, and walked about restlessly while he waited for the operator to call him back.

"I remember Roy telling me at the wedding reception that he'd talked to Vaizey. But he didn't say where or when. It could have been at County. It had no importance then—so I didn't ask."

Outside it had grown dark and the lights were coming on along Humboldt Avenue. Waiting now reminded her of waiting for that other call with Bill Randall. She shivered suddenly.

"Sometimes when I think of what happened, it frightens me!" she whispered. "Glen, couldn't she have been saved?"

He sat down beside her. "You mean at County? I've wondered about that too. Val—I don't know. Probably not."

"Because she refused the transfusion?"

"No. It was just too late when she was brought to the hospital."

"But if you'd been there? Or Bill?"

He felt weary. The things he had learned tonight had become a heavy weight on his mind. "I don't know, Val. Either of us would have attempted surgery. At once. So would Dr. Lindemann. He was the resident in charge of Emergency that night. But we'd had an earlier emergency. I operated with Lindemann. Then I rushed off to the wedding. Perhaps if I'd stayed—" He qualified that. It sounded boastful. He said, "Lindemann diagnosed the condition. But she was already dead."

"If only I'd been able to help her. But Carol was always so quiet, so reserved." Valerie sighed. "You just said that Dr. Lindemann didn't get there until after she was dead?"

"I left him in the Recovery Room with patients we'd treated surgically after a road accident. One of them was in a serious condition. He'd had an operation for a ruptured spleen. An intern admitted Carol and gave her initial treatment. He was prepared to transfuse her against her wishes, and take responsibility." He frowned, remembering Ward. "But Dr. Vaizey came in then. Vaizey is a resident. He took over, naturally—"

"And went on with the transfusion?"

"He examined her first."

"If Dr. Vaizey was the man, would she have recognized him? Surely she would have spoken to him. She knew she was dying."

He shook his head. He didn't want to believe what his accurate mind was forcing upon him now. He said slowly, "She was in coma when Dr. Vaizey examined her."

"I see!" She was staring at him suddenly. "Glen, did he diagnose the condition that killed Carol?"

"Yes! And he ordered the charge nurse to start the transfusion that Ward had prepared." He shrugged. "It was too late then!"

She frowned, considering that. "But she talked to Dr. Ward?"

"Yes."

"And Alden Vaizey was the man in charge. Why wasn't he *there* while she was still conscious? While she was able to talk to Dr. Ward?"

That was the question troubling him. "Dr. Vaizey couldn't know how serious it was until he examined her," he said quietly.

She moved closer to him, and he felt her shudder.

"Glen, suppose Alden Vaizey deliberately kept away until he saw she was unconscious? Until he knew she couldn't recognize him?"

Carew frowned, but he said nothing. He was remembering suddenly that Ward had said that Vaizey stopped him transfusing. That Vaizey had spoken to him sharply from the *doorway*. That was one of the reasons for Ward's anger. It *could* have been like that.

"That would be close to murder, Val." His voice was so low it was almost a whisper.

"That's the way I look at it. It would be murder! Murder to cover a scandal, murder to cover a mistake."

"No!" he said defensively.

"It's been done by men before. Murder to be rid of a woman who loved them. Murder to be rid of the embarrassment of a woman they'd made pregnant. If it was Alden Vaizey, I hope they execute him! Jail—that's too good for men like that!"

He stared at her silently. He couldn't force himself to believe that.

The ringing of the phone cut across his thoughts, and he got up quickly. She sat very still watching him. He came back slowly, his face older, more tired.

"Well?" she demanded.

"Vaizey came to see Roy Flagg at County. Roy showed him around the hospital. Roy says he was particularly interested in obstetrical anesthesia. They spent quite a lot of time in the obstetric wing. Roy wasn't with him all the time. Lindsay, our OB chief, asked Flagg to give a spinal anesthesia. Vaizey waited outside until it was over. Then they went back to the residence and had coffee."

"Then Alden Vaizey *was* at the hospital. He *could* have taken the drug."

"It's possible. Roy had just shown him around the wing. Nurses are in and out of the rooms on the maternity floor all the time. The drug—pitressin—would be in use frequently, not locked up. It would be risky—but he could have taken some. He could have slipped a few ampules into his pocket quickly."

"He *took* the drug!" she said vindictively.

"Proof that he had access to the drug isn't evidence at law that he took it."

"It's good enough for me!" she flashed back at him angrily. "Sometimes I think you just don't want to *know* that someone like Alden Vaizey, another *doctor*, did it!

106

Is that what's holding you back, Glen?"

"Nothing will hold me back once I'm sure!" He stood up.

"If you're ever sure," she said bitterly, as she watched him go to the door.

He turned. "Thanks for your help, Val. Good night."

Then he was gone. But the memory of those dark eyes black with anger that she had deliberately roused, stayed with her a long time. She doubted that she would ever see him again. Closing the door, she blamed herself.

CHAPTER TEN

THE Flying Ambulance plane, out of Calco on a mercy mission, droned steadily over ridges and deep valleys bright with fall coloring. Soon the leaves would drop, then snow would come to the high Nevada Sierras, making flying difficult. But right now the weather was perfect, with the shadow of the plane etched in black below them against a background of forest and sunlight.

There were two stretcher cases in the plane, each with almost identical fractures of the femur acquired in a road accident on the way home after what must have been quite a drinking spree in Charlesville, down on the edge of the desert. Dr. Glen Carew was taking them in now to Calco County Hospital for surgical treatment.

But the fractures had been reduced and the patients were reasonably comfortable under light sedation. They were brothers, sandy-haired, lean, with the dehydrated look of desert men. Both were smoking Carew's cigarettes, talking together in low voices, or joking occasionally with Max Addison, the burly pilot of the Cessna that served County as a flying ambulance.

In the seat next to the pilot, Glen Carew was staring at mountains far ahead that rose steeply to become a high plateau at the limit of vision.

In the back seat between the two stretchers, Dr. Alden Vaizey stared sullenly at Glen Carew's broad back. He had always hated flying, and he could find no logical reason why Glen Carew should have dragged him out on this comparatively unimportant pickup. The men in the stretchers were in no immediate need of surgery, or of an anesthesiologist. He had given them mild sedation on Carew's instructions, and he had helped Carew make the first reduction of the fractures at the ranch where they'd picked up the men. Now Carew would probably wait until the swelling subsided before he would attempt the repair that would hold the fracture permanently in its present reduction in each case.

Of course he could have been needed. If there'd been complications, infection, gangrene. . . .

But Carew had had another reason for bringing him on this trip, he was sure. There was no reason why Kathie Forrest, or any other nurse, could not have done what he had in assisting Carew.

He looked away from Carew in disgust, and stared out through the plexiglass, his handsome face sullen.

Why the hell did I ever come back to Calco? he thought bitterly.

At Chicago, he had fitted in. But here, except for Carew, the medical staff at County barely tolerated him. They didn't even bother to disguise their dislike. And now he'd been dragged out on an unimportant early morning pickup when he could have been still off duty back in the residence.

He had needed more sleep. Last night he had tried to persuade Dr. Jimmy Woldman to have a flutter at roulette down at the casino. Woldman had rejected his approach flatly. So he'd gone down to the casino alone and stayed too long. It didn't matter that he had dropped a few hundred dollars, but he had drunk too much whisky. He seemed to be doing that a lot lately.

Far ahead at the foot of the mountain range he glimpsed water suddenly, and recognized it. Almost at the same instant, he heard the sound of the Cessna's motors change from a steady beat to a flutter of sound that died abruptly.

"Blast!" Max Addison said.

109

Vaizey turned, startled. "What's wrong?"

"Electrical fault," Max Addison's deep voice said. He was bending over his controls, working at something outside Vaizey's field of vision. "I can fix it easily enough, but—"

"But what?" Carew asked.

"We're going to have to put her down while I do it. . . . There!"

In the cabin, after the silence of dead motors, the sound of their starting was disproportionately loud. Vaizey listened anxiously, aware that he was frightened. "Okay now?" he asked.

Max Addison shook his head with without looking around. "Not until I make the repair. Can't risk a dead prop over the mountains. There's a strip down here somewhere. Place called Cherry Lake. Charter planes fly in during the trout fishing season. Don't know what sort of condition the strip's in, though. It isn't used often. I'll call Calco Tower."

"The strip's okay," Vaizey said. "At least, the grass is short on it."

Addison turned his head, the speaker of the radio transmitter in his hand. "You know it?"

"I've got a cabin on the lake next to the strip," Vaizey said testily. "Of course I know it!"

"Been away, haven't you? Seen it lately? The grass could've grown, or there could be potholes?"

"I stayed down there for a couple of days before I started at County. I tell you it's *okay!* Why, a plane landed while I was there. Some fellows from Reno. I don't know much about flying, but they didn't seem to have any trouble." He glanced anxiously from Addison to Carew. "There's even a wind sock—"

Carew said, "How long before you started at County?"

"I came back the same morning. The plane I told you about could still be there. They said they were staying a couple of weeks. Fishing. They had a cabin and a boat not far from my place."

"We'll take a look," Addison said. He turned back to his controls. The motors sputtered and picked up again.

One of the men in the stretchers echoed Vaizey's fear.

110

"For crissake, get us down out of here, Max!" he said in a startled voice.

"It's safer up here than in some trucks I could mention, Pete," Addison retorted. "There's nothing to worry about. Not unless we tackled the mountains with an electrical fault. And we're not going to do that. If Cherry Lake strip's out, we can still make another strip I know a few miles farther west. Fasten your belt, Dr. Vaizey. Smokes out, everyone. Glen, you've plenty of time to check the stretchers."

Carew slipped out of his seat and came back, talking to his patients as he checked the straps that held them on the stretchers. Vaizey watched him nervously, his own stomach feeling tight against his safety belt. He did not offer to help.

"Calco Tower," Addison's calm voice said. "VA8 calling. We have a visual on Cherry Lake two miles east. About to make unscheduled landing Cherry Lake strip for minor electrical repair. VA8 over."

"VA8, Calco Tower." The voice of the Calco Tower operator sounded metallic in the cabin. "Roger. Report on landing. Over."

"Roger, Calco. . . ."

It sounded so matter-of-fact that a little of Vaizey's nervousness departed. He glanced down, and wet his lips with the tip of his tongue. The earth seemed spinning below him slowly as Addison banked. He could see the cabin, and the length of strip beside it with a plane parked at the far end where the wind sock pointed halfheartedly down the otherwise empty runway.

"You're as safe as though you were in bed," Carew said to one of the patients reassuringly. "Leg feel okay?"

"Damn near forgot it, Doc," he said, grinning. "Pete and me, we're just not used to planes. Trucks are our line. And like Max says, maybe not so safe at that—"

"Not when *you're* driving!" his brother said.

"How'd I know there was goin' to be a boulder slid down on that bend—"

"You were both lucky," Carew said. "You won't even limp for more than a few weeks."

He went back to his seat and Vaizey watched him clip his belt unconcernedly. He looked down again. The lake

111

was below them now, a smooth stretch of slightly blue water that stretched away toward a line of cliffs reaching up almost perpendicularly to become the mountains.

Alden Vaizey shivered and wet his lips. Addison was a good pilot. A very good pilot. He had been hearing stories about Max Addison's ability for years, but he found himself gripping the arms of his seat nevertheless.

"Looks fine," Addison said. "No trouble here. Smooth as asphalt. . . . Say, one of those guys has a fish."

Vaizey could see the boat on the edge of the lake, and two men in it looking up. One of them did have a fish— he could see the rod bending, the swirl where the fish broke water, before the boat passed beneath him and was gone.

He felt better suddenly. The plane was losing height in a smooth glide toward the pointing wind sock. The trees at the edge of the lake flicked past, and beyond the trees he glimpsed one of the fishermen starting the outboard motor. The Cessna touched and ran down the strip, slowing as Addison braked, turning slightly across the strip toward the cabins on the lake side.

Vaizey saw his own cabin, a solid log structure larger than any of the others, gliding toward him. He stared at it as the plane stopped.

"We're down," Addison said cheerfully. "And no trouble. Well, it's always better to be sure. Take me twenty minutes to fix the fault, and I'm going to need a little room to move about. Glen, why don't you and Dr. Vaizey stretch your legs while I do that? You can smoke outside. Just loosen the straps for the boys—they're not going to get up and run away. How about that?"

"I could use some sunshine," Carew said. He unclipped his seat belt and stood up. He came back to the stretchers and loosened the straps. "You boys will have to do without a smoke till we're airborne again. But we'll think of you." He glanced at Vaizey. "Coming?"

Alden Vaizey shook his head. "Thanks, I'll stay here."

"Sorry, Doc," Addison said. "Like I said, I need the room. Got some stuff I need stashed away back there."

"Okay," Vaizey said grudgingly.

Outside, the cabin stood solidly against the back-

112

ground of lake and trees. Vaizey frowned. They seemed almost to be pushing him toward it. But that couldn't be.

He followed Glen Carew reluctantly out through the door and down the steps. The cabin looked just the same as it always had. Quiet, peaceful. A retreat from examinations, from the strain of internship, the Chicago residency, the insistence of his uncle that he take an active part in the running of the stores. . . .

The cabin had always been a place of escape.

Sometimes now he wondered why he hadn't been satisfied with commercial life. Then he could have come here more often.

He had had a lot of good times behind those log walls. There had been parties, girls. He had meant to bring the Montez girl down here, only—

"Cigarette?" Carew was holding out a pack to him. He followed the direction of Vaizey's gaze. "Say, that's really a nice cabin. I could sure use a place like that myself when the trout are rising. Solid and comfortable. By the way, Vaizey, which one is yours?"

"That's it," he said curtly. He drew on the cigarette. He began to feel the need of a drink suddenly, and remembered the well-stocked cupboard inside. But he wasn't going to invite Carew in there.

"Should be plenty of room. You have a boat, of course?"

"There's a shed on the edge of the water. You can see the slips." Carew, he decided, was obviously hinting to be taken inside. He was frightened suddenly, with an unreasoning fear that made him feel cold. He needed a drink worse than ever. The breakdown, the landing here was starting to take on a pattern that appalled him.

"Is something the matter, Dr. Vaizey?" Carew's voice asked mildly.

"Of course not!"

"You look pale."

Vaizey looked away, avoiding Carew's steady gaze. He was finding it strange that he had often thought Carew's eyes too soft for a man's eyes. He had been wrong about that. They were almost black now, with a hard brilliance that masked expression. Almost sinister.

"I'm afraid I'm not used to planes," he said nervously. "Landing, I felt a little airsick."

"Airsickness is partly psychological, you know. Worry . . . fear, can help cause it."

"I don't believe I was either worried or afraid up there, Dr. Carew," he said angrily.

"Up there—no. You were calm enough. A personal worry then?"

"I didn't say that."

Carew smiled. "No, of course you didn't. It was just your color." He looked at the cabin. "I like a stone fireplace and chimney, but you have to know your stone, of course. Bricks are a little unusual in log cabins around here. Those are handmade, aren't they?"

"My father had them molded and hand-bolted." He put out his hand to his forehead. The coldness he had felt was sweat. He wiped it away with a handkerchief, aware that Carew's eyes followed the movement. "You know, you could be right about my color. I don't feel so good right now." He flipped the cigarette away. "I think I'll lean against the plane until Addison is ready."

Carew glanced at his watch. "Well, Max said twenty minutes, and he's always accurate. Mind if I take a look at those bricks?"

"Of course not." He wondered if Carew had noticed his hesitation, but Carew's expression gave him no indication. Why did Carew seem so insistent on seeing the damned cabin?

"Log cabins always interest me," Carew said. "I'll fill in the rest of the time by talking to those men who were fishing. Looks as though they're coming in to see what's the matter."

"Eh? Oh yes, of course, Doctor. I'm okay here."

"Didn't you say they arrived while you were here?"

"Yes, I did."

"That must have been nice for you."

"Nice for me?" What the hell was Carew driving at now? Vaizey frowned uneasily. "I don't understand."

Carew smiled—a cold smile that held neither mirth nor friendliness. "Sorry! I formed the impression you were alone down here. But naturally, you'd bring some company."

114

"No. I was tired. I came down alone. I— just couldn't be bothered with anyone. There are times when I'm quite satisfied with my own company, Doctor."

"I'll leave you to it, then," Carew said. "I noticed one of them taking a photo of the plane as we landed. Maybe I can get a photo of the lake and your cabin from them. You know how tourists are—always taking casual snapshots when they're on holiday. Some of them might be interesting."

"I never noticed them taking photographs," Alden Vaizey said, frowning. "Wait, I'll come with you." He didn't want Carew talking to those two men. He didn't remember a camera, but there *could* have been!

"Don't bother, if you don't feel up to it," Carew said.

"No, really! I'm all right now. I'll come."

"You still look rather peaked."

"I've just remembered there's some brandy in the cabin. Look, why don't we go inside and have a quick drink? I think I'll feel the better for it. You can examine the bricks at your leisure then. Perhaps you'll find them interesting. The guy who baked them was part Shoshone."

Vaizey glanced at the men walking up from the lake. Neither seemed to be carrying a camera, but they could have left it in the boat. He watched their indecision as they cleared the fringe of trees, and for a moment he thought they were going to walk toward the cabin.

"Come on," he said hastily. "Let's get out of the sun."

Carew nodded. "Just as you say, Doctor."

Walking toward the cabin door, fumbling for his key case, Alden Vaizey watched the two men turn away toward the plane. He breathed easier. He inserted the key in the door, and ushered Carew inside quickly.

The cabin had the faintly musty smell of a holiday cottage seldom used and close to water. The living room was huge and comfortably furnished.

Carew glanced around.

"Like it?" Vaizey asked. But Carew wasn't looking at the fireplace. His eyes were studying the bedrooms opening from the living room. "The bricks are red and yellow, made from different clays. The brickmaker tried blue clay, but I believe the color baked out of them. I don't remember much about it. I was only a boy then."

115

"You did some fishing when you were down here, of course?" Carew was examining a rod on pegs above the mantel.

"I—well, no, I didn't. Mostly I lazed about. Why?"

"The binding of the ferrules has dried out. It's been a long while since this one was used."

"I keep mine put away. It's in good condition, Doctor. Scotch and water? I'm afraid there's no ice. The refrigerator only gets started when I come down here. And that isn't often."

"No, thanks. Right now, I don't feel like drinking. But don't mind me."

"I won't!" Vaizey poured three fingers of brandy, added a splash of water, and drank it quickly.

Carew was moving about the big room. "I see you keep an emergency bag here." He had noticed one on a chair. He stopped and looked at it. The bag bore the words, "Alden Vaizey, M.D." in gold lettering upon its black surface. He read them out aloud.

"I'd forgotten that," Vaizey said. "I should have put it away." He was coming across the room suddenly. "I'll do that now."

But Carew had opened the bag and was looking inside, his face expressionless.

"I said I'd take that!"

"Yes, of course." Carew closed it and handed it to him. "I see you have a hypodermic?"

"And a stethoscope and other instruments. I even keep a few standard drugs about the place. Or used to. But as I said, I haven't used this place much in years. This is an old diagnostic set I bought as an intern. But in a place like this, you never know when you might need it. Accidents happen. People fall sick when they're vacationing just the same as any place else."

"Oh? And you had a patient?"

"No, of course not!" He looked at Carew angrily.

"I notice the hypodermic has been used recently," Carew persisted. "The other things are thick with dust, but the syringe has been sterilized."

"Phenobarbital!" Vaizey said quickly. "Do I have to confess I couldn't sleep and gave myself an injection? I

116

can assure you I'm not addicted to barbiturates, Dr. Carew."

"The signs of addiction are easy enough to find, if they're there. No, that wasn't what I was thinking."

Vaizey laughed. "Really, Dr. Carew—sometimes I find you a little difficult to understand. You're acting as though —well, as though I had something to hide! There are cupboards here, but they're empty of skeletons. I thought you were interested in brickwork?"

He reached for the brandy bottle. Pouring himself another drink, he was aware that his hand shook. It took effort to correct that.

"I'm wondering what you are addicted to," Carew said. "There are a lot of cigarette butts stained with lipstick. A dark shade. Maybe you are addicted to brunettes."

Vaizey put the glass down. "I don't know what you're trying to say, Dr. Carew," he said with forced calm. "But I resent your tone. I brought you in here to—"

"To look at bricks," Carew said grimly. "But I'm looking at other things."

He had thought a lot about this moment, and he hadn't been sure that he could go through with it—that he could bring himself to try to destroy this man glaring at him now, his face pale and angry. Even in his own anger, he had wondered about that. But now he knew that he could. His mind kept picturing what he was sure had happened . . . the girl coming.

He continued, "Like a syringe. A needle. Towels, drying over there on a rack. Why so many towels, Dr. Vaizey? Were you frightened you'd bleed to death when the needle pricked you? When you injected phenobarbital to make you sleep? Did you hemorrhage?"

"You're talking damned nonsense, Carew!"

"Did you hemorrhage?"

"Nobody hemorrhaged, damn you! Towels grow damp here, and smell musty. I hung them there to dry."

"Then you wouldn't mind if I took one back for a lab check, would you? For blood?"

"If you find blood trace, it's mine!"

"Sure!" Carew said. "You cut yourself shaving with

117

the electric shaver hanging over there on the shelf. And the lipstick?"

"So I had a girl here. I wouldn't expect you to understand that. Her name's Montez, she works in the store—"

"Nita Montez? You brought *her* down here?"

"Yes, I did! So what?"

"You're lying, Vaizey. You intended to bring Nita Montez, but you phoned and called it off. You brought Carol Vincent instead! You injected her with the syringe and needle in the case. You injected her with four shots of pitressin you stole from the OB wing at County while Roy Flagg was showing you around!"

"You're crazy! Carol Vincent's the girl who died of a tubal pregnancy. I never saw her until they wheeled her into the Emergency Room."

He was staring at Carew now, white to the lips.

"You knew her in Chicago, Vaizey. You made love to her there."

"No!"

"She became pregnant, although neither of you knew it then. She sold her shop and came here to be near you. She knew you intended to take up an appointment at County that your uncle had tied up for you with pink ribbons. But while she waited for you to come, she found she was pregnant—"

"Take care how you accuse me, Carew! Ever heard of criminal libel? You're defaming me without proof."

"Am I? Maybe you just made love the night she came here with you, Vaizey. But the next morning, somewhere around say ten or eleven o'clock—you injected her. And you did it without a proper examination. You missed the fact that it wasn't a normal pregnancy, that it was a tubal conception. *You damned fool!* You couldn't face that, you bastard! You left her near a telephone booth to call the ambulance—"

"I won't listen to any more!" Vaizey cried, his face working. "I won't! You've got no proof! None!"

He turned toward the door. Max Addison's bulk filled the doorway.

"Maybe this is what you want, Glen," Addison said grimly. "I've seen better color shots, but it'll do. They took it the day they arrived here. They took it from the

118

plane. It's a shot of the cabin and the lake. He's standing near the door, and there's a girl with him. It isn't Nita Montez. I know Nita. This girl is smaller. She's wearing a dress with a floral pattern on it—green!"

"She was wearing it when they picked her up off the floor of the telephone booth," Carew said grimly. "And when you stood at the door of the Emergency Room waiting for her to lapse into coma before you came nearer, Vaizey. While you waited for her to die!"

"No!" He could see it all now. The faked landing here. Carew's suspicious searching. The photo. . . .

Alden Vaizey exploded into violent action abruptly. He swung a punch at Carew, hitting him high up on the cheekbone, then he was trying to wrest the photo from Addison.

Carew caught his arms, but he wrenched away, cursing, swinging his fists wildly, his face a mask of fear and hatred.

Addison, moving in quickly to help as he stuffed the photo into his shirt pocket, saw Glen Carew's hand close and hit. He slid to a stop, grinning. Vaizey went over backward, taking a chair with him. He lay there, dazed. The hand that he put to his mouth came away red.

"That's . . . not . . . evidence!" he panted from the floor. "You can't prove any of that . . . in court!"

"I'm going to try," Carew promised him grimly "And right now the police are checking in Chicago. Someone must have seen you with Carol Vincent there. But one thing's sure—you're through, Vaizey. You'll never practice medicine again. Not as an anesthesiologist, not as anything. I'll see to that!"

"A little harder, and someone would be practicing medicine on *him,*" Addison said. "You just about knocked his mustache off! I'll pick him up, if you want to try again."

Glen Carew blew on his stinging knuckles, and looked at the man moaning on the floor, a thin trickle of blood staining the front of his white shirt.

"Just get him into the plane, Max," he said. "I don't want to touch him. But get him out of here!"

119

CHAPTER ELEVEN

VALERIE CASSIDY hadn't been sure
that he would come back, but he was standing outside the
apartment, looking at her as she opened the door. It was
late at night, and she had slipped only a light robe over
her nightgown.

"Glen, why are you here?"

"I came to tell you that you were right and I was
wrong," he said wearily. "It *was* Alden Vaizey."

She looked at him silently for a long moment. "Come
in. You need a drink."

She closed the door behind her, and went quickly to
the kitchenette to pour the drinks. She said over her
shoulder as he walked about restlessly, "Was it—that
sticky?"

"Bad enough. There were all kinds of inquiries. The
Medical Examiner's Office, the police." He added after a
while, "He's had it. He'll never practice medicine again."

"Don't feel sorry for him now, Glen," she thought.
"Don't measure him by the yardstick of your own feeling
about medicine."

She said aloud, "Did he admit it?"

"His uncle was there with a lawyer. They decided to
plead guilty to the charge of administering the pitressin
to cause an abortion. It'll probably be manslaughter. I
don't know. I'm a doctor, Val, not a lawyer."

"They should charge him with first-degree homicide! Take away more than just the practice of medicine and a few years of his time," she said viciously. "They should take away his life!"

Carew said nothing.

"And Uncle Andrew posts bail, and he doesn't go to jail?"

"After the trial, he'll go to jail."

She could hear him walking about, and the sound of his footsteps were not as firm as she remembered.

He said inconsequentially, "He said he loved her."

"He said he loved her? Good God! Does he call that *love?"* She had come out of the alcove and was staring at him, ice poised in the spoon in her hand.

"That's what he said."

"Carol loved him, and he—!" She set the drinks on the low coffee table. She drew up her slim legs, sitting with her knees turned sideways, like a small girl at a doll's tea party.

He saw for the first time that she wore a nightgown, that her feet were bare.

He came and sat beside her. "Yes. Carol loved him, and he said he only did it because she insisted. He had wanted to marry her. But she didn't want it like that. She wanted a fresh start. Then marriage."

"Glen, you don't believe that?" she gasped. "That beast is playing for sympathy. And she isn't here to deny it."

"No, I can't believe it, Val. Maybe because it's beyond my comprehension. But maybe I don't want to believe it, either. Like the way I was when you were so sure he was the man . . ."

"But after you left here, when you thought about it, you went after him? It *was* you who was responsible for his—arrest?"

"Yes," he said wearily. "It was me."

"Tell me about it," she said soberly. "You'll feel better then. And so will I."

"It isn't pleasant," he said, remembering.

She touched his arm. "Doctors are just men too, Glen. There must be good and bad. There has to be. And Alden Vaizey is—bad. . . . I keep thinking of Carol. Is that what you're thinking of, too?"

"Val, I've studied medicine, but I'm afraid I don't know much about motives that could drive a doctor to—that."

"Don't think of him as a doctor, Glen," she said with compassion as she studied his face. "Don't!"

"It could have worked out for them. If he loved her—"

She shook her head. "He didn't love her. If he had, they would have married, and nothing Carol could say would have changed *that*. Could a girl who loved a man refuse him marriage and a child?"

He turned away, confused.

"Tell me about it," she said gently.

He started speaking then, "After I left you last night, I talked to Max Addison. We set a trap for him. . . ."

Across the town as he talked, she could see the lights of County Hospital. There were always lights there, she knew, but that was a life she neither knew nor understood.

All she knew was that it seemed to go on calmly, inexorably. Never tiring, or stopping. Life and death and service to the sick. They saved life when they could. They fought death. And sometimes they lost. And it went on and on. There was no end to it. It was not quite human, even though the components were human.

Listening to Glen Carew's quiet voice she found herself remembering Bill Randall and his word to her on another night like this.

"To heal sometimes, to relieve often, to console always."

Bill Randall had said that, and now in her own way she was consoling Glen Carew. An inner knowledge told her that he needed her like this, beside him, listening. As a wife might listen, without the need for possession. Without possession. . . .

It would have been easier to give him her body, but in *this* there was deeper satisfaction.

She moved closer. Became absorbed. . . .

Behind one set of lighted windows in the hospital, Dr. Stanley Prentice talked earnestly, driving home viciously points that none of the watching faces around the Board table could deny. He was not sure how long he had talked, but he knew that he was hot beneath the lights above the table, and that his notes lay neglected before him.

He was closing his speech now, watching the Board Chairman as he sat at the head of the table staring down fixedly. At first Andrew Vaizey had had plenty to say. And so had other members of the Board.

But slowly, as Dr. Prentice talked, all that had changed. Now Andrew Vaizey sat silently, gloomily staring at notes he had planned to use but had not used, as the tide of opinion swung against him.

". . . In conclusion," Prentice said, "I must repeat, gentlemen, that when you take the choice of highly trained medical staff out of the jurisdiction of your Medical Superintendent and his service chiefs, you leave the hospital open to criticism by the Medical Examiner's Office. As it has been criticized. You leave yourselves and this hospital open to rebuke by the American Hospital Accreditation Commission. As it will be rebuked. And we have always been very proud of our accreditation here at County. In the medical profession, and among the millions of Americans who depend on hospital service when they're injured or sick, that means something.

"But one of the platforms of accreditation is the rigid set of standards that doctors must achieve before they can be employed as residents. A doctor must be qualified, and he must be ethical. With all due respect to the members of this Board as individuals, I say that no layman is qualified to decide that on either count. In the first place, he does not have the technical knowledge. In the second, he does not have access to channels of confidential information which are available to the Medical Superintendent of any accredited hospital and his service chiefs."

Dr. Prentice looked around at their intent faces. "Tonight I've had to say a lot of bitter things. But *you* made that necessary, gentlemen, individually and collectively. If you disagree with me, I shall submit my resignation as a matter of course. That's all, gentlemen."

He sat down in the midst of a subdued buzz of inaudible comment that stilled suddenly as a man across the table spoke.

"I'd like to ask Dr. Prentice a question."

Andrew Vaizey did not look up. "Granted!"

"Dr. Prentice, are we to presume that these, ah—confidential channels of information you mention, were available to you in the case of, ah—Dr. Vaizey?"

"They were."

"In that case, if the appointment had come to you in the normal way with other applications—would you have recommended Dr. Vaizey?"

"I would *not!*"

"Not if, say, ah—the number of applications had been limited, and you found that the medical qualifications of the applicants were equal?"

"No!"

"Your opposition would have been on ethical grounds, I take it?"

"Yes."

"Which you cannot divulge here?"

"That's right."

"Thank you, Doctor." The Board member looked at the Chairman. "If Dr. Vaizey already had ethical strikes against him before he came to us, ah—highly recommended, I can only assume the Chair knew of this. I think I've made my point, gentlemen. And I feel sure that in view of this, our Chairman may have something to say."

It had been neatly done. The next move obviously would be a vote of no confidence in the Chairman. The Board member was already looking for support while he waited, and getting it. But Dr. Prentice felt no exultation as he looked at Andrew Vaizey. Instead, although he had instigated it, he felt sorry for him. Andrew Vaizey looked older than his years suddenly. He stood up wearily, leaning his weight on his hands against the tabletop as he looked around at them.

"Yes," he said. "I have something to say to you. The name of Vaizey has long been associated with this hospital. I had hoped it would continue for a long time. I wanted my nephew on the medical staff. I wanted—" He broke off. "That doesn't matter now. My nephew is no longer practicing medicine. And I—no longer wish to be associated with Calco County Hospital. Gentlemen, I hereby resign from the position of Board Chairman, and from this Board."

"I move that Mr. Vaizey's resignation be accepted."
The man who had questioned Prentice was on his feet
at once.

"I second that!"

"All those in favor?"

"Aye!"

Andrew Vaizey listened to that deep, resonant chorus.
He shook his head a little dazedly, then he gathered the
papers before him, and walked out heavily.

Dr. Prentice listened to the brief closure, to the mo-
tion that set a date for the extraordinary meeting that
would elect a new chairman. The meeting was declared
closed, and Miss Hilder picked up her notebooks and
went out into her office. Men spoke to Dr. Prentice; he
answered them. A page had turned. A new page was
opening. Nothing like that would happen again.

But Dr. Prentice could not forget Andrew Vaizey's
face as he saw him gradually, mercilessly defeated. There
was no joy in it for him. No joy at all.

Miss Hilder came back when the others had gone.
"You must be awfully tired, Doctor." She smiled. "I've
made some coffee. Strong and black—the way you like
it. Shall I bring it in now, or will you come through into
the office?"

"I don't want it."

She waited for comment. There was always comment
after a Board meeting. And when it didn't come, she lost
a little of her pert assurance. She said tentatively,
"Well—?"

"Well, what?" he snapped.

"We won, didn't we? That was what you wanted."

"Get the devil out of here!" he snarled.

He watched her retreat. The door of the board room
banged shut. He felt a little better. He started to smile.
He had never known Miss Hilder to bang a door before.

Through the open window of the board room, he could
see the main entrance to the hospital, and as he watched,
a group of nurses streamed out, going off duty. He
watched them hurrying toward the residence across the
lawns. Their hurry told him that this was the evening shift
going off duty. They were tired girls now, needing rest. It
would soon be midnight. But the hospital would continue

to function with clockwork precision as other nurses took their places—as other residents and interns took the place of the young men in white coats straggling out, to hunch their shoulders against the cold of an autumn night and walk toward their own residence, hands thrust deep in their trouser pockets.

This was his hospital, and he was going to run it as he always had—precisely, efficiently, with the best damned staff he could get.

He stood up and pushed his chair back. He looked in the outer office.

"Iris, where's that damned coffee?"

Miss Hilder looked up, startled, from where she was putting her notebooks angrily but precisely in their drawer. "You said—"

"Don't I always have coffee with you after a Board meeting?"

"Yes, but—"

"I think I'll have cream in it tonight. Yes, I will. A sort of celebration. Bring yours in and join me, eh? Well—?"

"Yes, of course, Doctor," she said happily.

"That's better," he said. "We won, didn't we?"

Driving in through the high scroll-iron front gates of the hospital, Glen Carew slowed for the group of nurses and acknowledged the quick wave of one who recognized him. He found himself looking automatically for Kathie Forrest, but she was not among them.

He eased into one of the marked spaces reserved for doctors' cars outside the residence, and lit a cigarette. He felt better now. Talking to Valerie Cassidy had eased the tensions that had built in a long and difficult day. At the door of her apartment, he had given her a quick, friendly kiss. But that was all. Valerie Cassidy would soon fade from his mind.

He looked up at the windows of the nurses' residence and thought in relief of Kathie Forrest. The third window on the first floor was hers, he knew. And as though she sensed his presence, he saw her as a shadow against the drawn curtains briefly as she crossed the room.

Her light went out abruptly then, leaving him alone.

Glen Carew sighed. He parked the car.

Tomorrow, he and Kathie would be working together again. Tomorrow, he would find the opportunity to talk to her about what had happened today.

Only he wouldn't tell her of the way he had felt briefly tonight about Val Cassidy, because that was something he couldn't explain. They were two people who had been drawn together in common anger. They weren't friends. They couldn't be—and they'd parted now.

Or had they *parted?* Had there ever really been anything between them? He was aware now only of a deep content that had come of talking to her like that, of her nearness while he talked. . . .

But nothing more. There never had been anything more.

In a few days, unless they met by accident, even the clear memory of her face that his mind held now would be gone. And with Val Cassidy, it would be the same way.

Walking back to the entrance to the residence, he glanced up at a darkened window. It would never be like that with Kathie Forrest. Never.

He looked up, smiling, before he ran up the steps. "Tomorrow," he thought. "Tomorrow, Kathie . . ."

And the thought was pleasant, even though she might still be angry.